Alistair Mackenzie
and the
International Jihadist

Ian Grant

Alistair Mackenzie and the International Jihadist

By **Ian Grant**

Published by Author Way Limited through CreateSpace
Copyright 2015 author

This book has been brought to you by -

Discover other Author Way Limited titles at - http://www.authorway.net
Or to contact the author mailto:info@authorway.net

ISBN: 1517180708
ISBN-13:   978-1517180706

I would like dedicate this book to Elaine and Gerry Mann and thank them for all their help and encouragement

.

CHAPTER 1

Cutting the throat of an infidel was going to be the highlight of Yousef's week.

All was ready. Schneider was suitably prepared in his orange Guantanamo-type jumpsuit. The black flag had been unfurled and carefully attached with bluetac to a bare concrete wall. The camera was fixed to a tripod. Set up on the floor a couple of feet in front, was a plain, wooden box, on which to push Schneider's head. All had been carefully positioned in readiness.

All Yousef had to do now was to wash, dress and pray, before ordering Schneider be brought into the large room. It was immediately adjacent to the one in which he had been chained to the floor, on and off, for the last eighteen months.

Yousef felt the cool, clear water run through his fingers. Soon there would be blood, warm blood that would also cleanse and anoint him in the eyes of the prophet.

Now physically and ritually cleansed, Yousef pulled from his back-pack two pairs of tight underpants to wear under his black robe. On a previous occasion he had started to get an erection in the moments before the drawing of the knife along his victim's neck. He did not know why he found the taking of life in this way to be arousing, but with the world watching the video, Yousef didn't want to share what he saw as a weakness with everyone who watched.

As Schneider was led, his hands bound half crawling, half walking to his fate, Yousef spoke in English, in his soft Belfast accent, raising his arms in a very theatrical way.

He demanded, "Bring me the holy blade of death for this infidel."

The words had been carefully chosen. Yousef had used them before and now relished this opportunity to say them again.

Schneider had been through all this several times before. Mock executions were one of the ways his guards amused themselves between endless hours of boredom, military type training and daily prayer. Regular beatings, starvation and sleep deprivation had all formed a part of his existence since the Toyota Land-Cruiser in which he was travelling, was stopped on the hot and blindingly dusty road to Aleppo, by what looked like a police roadblock, all those months ago. He'd been with Aldo the photographer and Mohammed his driver and interpreter

Yousef stood well above the other Jihadists both physically, as a tall slim man of six foot four, and because of his ability, need even, to shed blood in the name of his beliefs. As a young boy, he wanted to become a famous actor. His undiagnosed dyslexia gave him an undeserved reputation amongst his peers as being stupid. The constant name calling and rejection grew a deep seated anger that went to the core of his personality. Several incidents involving cruelty and physical harm to animals, sometimes to his school friends and later to a teacher, made people wary. Even many of his close family sought to isolate him to the point where all of his early ambitions were permanently spoiled by others, at least in his opinion.

Schneider was made to bow as if in Muslim prayer. His head bent low. He was especially uncomfortable because of his relentless back pain. A few days after his capture, while taunting his sexuality, his guards had roughly pushed several inches of the barrel of a Kalashnikov rifle into his rectum shouting, "You like this? This is what you like! We will make it come for you, with a bullet, filthy spy."

The ensuing blood loss and infection had damaged all the muscles in his lower back causing him a permanent throbbing pain when kneeling. A droplet of sweat ran down Schneider's brow. He noticed that Yousef was wearing the steel, blue-faced, Omega watch snatched from him when he was blindfolded at the start of his capture. He also now noticed something new. A strong carbolic smell coming from a bucket of soapy water and a mop left leaning against the wall a couple of metres to the left of the black flag.

This could be it, he thought.

Schneider did not have long to wait.

"How do I look?" asked Yousef, "Is there plenty of power in the battery?

"O.K. Start the camera now."

As Schneider's eyes became locked into a thousand yard stare, Yousef pulled a plain, long-handled, seventeen inch, boning knife out of its leather scabbard. It was of the kind you would find in every butchers shop east of Istanbul. He held the knife with a straight arm; then with an almost effortless movement of his right elbow, Schneider's dreams of returning home to his husband and family finally ended; his lifeless body now slumped in ruin on the hard concrete floor. All the public appeals from his husband Paul and his friends and family had made no impact on Yousef and his beliefs.

"God is great and so are the avengers of the holy soil of Islam," said Yousef as he read from his prepared text. "This act was caused by you when you entered our land and defiled our brothers at Abu Graib. Now we will bring this avenging to your land, in the heart of the great Satan that you have made in America.

"You, who worship a cross, must now await your rewards. We, your avengers, are on our way to deliver the mercy of Allah to your Godless land!"

Yousef rambled on for another fifteen minutes to the point when even paid professional C.I.A. viewers of the tape began to lose interest.

CHAPTER 2

2236 Silverdale Crest, Upper Saddle River, New Jersey was built in the American Colonial style that was very popular for luxury, private residences constructed in suburbia in the late 1960's. A large, graceful and well-balanced detached building with an aluminium finish, crafted to look like weatherboard, gave the home the appearance of a huge dolls house. Standing in almost a quarter of an acre of mostly wooded gardens at the end of a long, curved cull-de- sac, the house was quite well known locally. The tall, white, flag pole to the extreme right of the property not only held aloft the classic patriotic red, white and blue stars and stripes, but on certain occasions displayed the blue and white St. Andrew's cross of Scotland, giving away the birthplace of the head of the family, Alistair Mackenzie.

Alistair had only ever worked for one employer, Ford Motor Co. Growing up on the south side of Glasgow he had excelled at school. From there received a scholarship to St. Andrew's University where he gained degrees in Science and Engineering. His interest in all things mechanical led to a first job as an Area Sales Manager looking after dealerships in the East of Scotland. As his career developed Alistair went on to postings in Dagenham, England and Cologne, Germany before climbing the corporate ladder in

Dearborn. His latest job as Vice President of product marketing (Lincoln, Mercury Division), working out of the National Marketing office in New York City was, he felt, the biggest stepping stone opportunity of his seventeen years with the firm. He was determined to let nothing stand in his way from making it a complete success.

07.25 on the crowded Monday morning commuter train from New Jersey to New York, Alistair Mackenzie started his working week. "Oh, Hello George, I was going to call you today anyway. You okay? What's up?" There was a long pause. "Yes, Oh, I'm sorry to hear that. If it's a matter of money we could discuss it. Oh, I see, and you're absolutely sure you want to do this. I will contact H.R. on your behalf. As you're going to another motor manufacturer I have to ask you to call into the L.A. office today and hand in your laptop, I Pad, security pass, business cards and mobile phone. I hope you enjoy your garden leave for the next four weeks. As for me, my schedule just doubled thanks to your news. You can still run the demonstrator car but try to keep the mileage down. Is your personal email still the same? Right."

07.55. "Hi Darling; bad news I'm afraid. I'm not going to make Jamie's school play next week. George just resigned and I'll have to go out west and cover his key accounts for the launch of the new Mercury Coupe. No, I know, but there's really no one else. I've already lost Mandy; she's on a management training course in Florida and we've cancelled the launch once already.

You remember I told you when three of the six test cars got a seized wheel bearing in cold weather, testing over in Sweden, a couple of months ago? Yeah, I'm sorry too. See you tonight. Love you, Bye."

08.15 335 Madison Avenue, NYC.

Alistair loved the location of his New York office. Not only was it in the very heart of New York City and only a brisk walk from Penn Station. It had a Starbucks coffee shop on the ground floor and, as headquarters for Bank of America, there was a wall of ATM machines, meaning he never had to queue to take out cash. The Wi-Fi was super-fast in every corner of the building. Sipping his favourite hot coffee with a dash of cinnamon, Alistair checked his Rolex. Good, he thought, Bernice, his angel of a P.A. would be in by now.

"Bernice, Hi, good morning. I'm downstairs nursing a coffee and a sore ear from my wife. Did you see the email I sent about George? Yeah, tell me about it. I'll be upstairs in ten but could you look out all of George's launch party dates? Yeah, when and where; oh and try to work out a plan for me to drop in instead. You'll do that? Great. Ten minutes then."

George's West coast patch was one of the largest areas geographically for Ford product marketing with dealerships long-spaced and sometimes having many miles of rugged country roads in between. Alistair realised that starting from New York it was going to be a real challenge, but with Bernice on his side a plan would soon emerge for him to follow.

CHAPTER 3

Yousef pulled his shiny, new, red, slim-line Sony laptop out from his back-pack and began to watch himself on YouTube. Transferring to CNN, BBC and other world news networks he was most satisfied that his work was reaching a huge audience. Time for some entertainment, he thought, as he returned to YouTube for a little inspiration. Typing in the word 'plot' he meandered through a long series of video options. This looks good, he thought, as he expanded the screen to watch "Secrets of Area 51." It turned out to be a very predictable story of how the U.S. government covered up its secret Blackhawk testing programme, blaming the massive security cordon on the huge public interest in aliens and flying saucers. This was also the reason given for the large numbers of troops and scientists stationed in the area. And then they said something that made Yousef sit up. "I guess, next to the White House, area 51 is the best known address in America."

Yousef typed in 'Area 51 United States location' into Google.

Area 51 is located in the southern portion of Nevada in the western United States, 83 miles (134 km) north-northwest of Las Vegas. Situated at its centre, on the southern shore of Groom Lake, is a large military airfield.

His next Google was "Groom lake Military

airfield."

Overwhelmed by the amount of information and speculation on offer, Yousef took note of one recurring aspect of the stories. Each time anyone strayed close enough to the perimeter, a couple of army security men were sent out to investigate the incursion. For Yousef this was like the chickens leaving the coup to go and look at the fox.

Almost immediately he had a plan.

Get to area 51

Buy a bracket to attach his video recorder to a car

Acquire guns and body armour

Get something or someone to bring the soldiers in close

Kill some guards and film it happening

Get home and post the video under the title, "Americans you are the real aliens."

Oh, and 7, become the most famous man in the World.

At times like this, Yousef turned to his old friend Mohammed. Mohammed had known him from the start. They had trained together in Yemen and he was still proving himself very useful. A recent example of this was when he delivered Schneider and his camera man right into their hands.

"Mohammed, how would I get to Las Vegas?" asked Yousef

"It is against our beliefs to gamble, but if you feel the need, Schneider had a few euros and some dollars which I kept, and a pack of cards that could still be retrieved from the trash."

"No, Mohammed, I'm serious! How can I get there?"

"Well, for a start you will need an American or European Passport. There is no point in looking for a forgery. Too easy to detect and anyway a real one is easy to get. The infidels joke that we all look alike to them. All we need to do is get one of our brothers in America or England who does not have a passport to apply for one using your photograph. They rely on birth certificates and babies as you know don't get their fingerprints taken, so it could be anyone. They post us the passport and you are in business."

"But what about the flying?" asked Yousef.

Mohammed squeezed his chin with his right hand in a gesture showing deep thought. Then pushed back his thick black hair from his sweating brow and began to make a quiet buzzing whistle through the wide gap in his front teeth as he pondered the idea.

"Where you are coming from is more important almost than where you are going. I would suggest you travel from here to Dubai on a British Passport. You will get lost in that crowded place full of western pigs and parasites. From there, on to Vilnius in Lithuania, and from Lithuania to Dublin in Ireland, where you either get an Irish passport to go with your accent or a U.S. one to complete your journey."

"Why Lithuania?" asked Yousef, looking puzzled.

"Since they joined the Euro, the country has been full of foreigners attracted by investment opportunities. The airports are handling twenty times the traffic with only a few old Russian-trained guards on the border posts. No one will notice you coming in from Dubai to Vilnius and you can then travel to a small airport out of the city and get on the crowded, Ryanair budget flight direct to Dublin."

"Okay. I get that bit, so why Dublin?"

"The airport at Swords, near Dublin, is one of only a handful in the world that has U.S. Customs based within the airport. If you have a U.S. or Irish passport you can enter U.S. territory even before you leave Ireland, it makes for a super quick, smooth arrival at J.F.K, especially if you are travelling on to L.A. using an internal Flight.

"Would you like me to come with you?" asked Mohammed, his eyes burning with excitement.

"No, but start to look and see if we have any friends in western United States who can help me on the ground. We will also need a lot of funds from our supporters who own the T.V. station in London."

"My cousins Achmed and his sister Noor work for a millionaire in a place called Holmby Hills, Los Angeles. We call them the Beverley hillbillies because they filmed those old shows only three streets away from where they now live. Ronald Reagan used to be another neighbour. Come to think about it, Achmed is a lot shorter than you but he could easily pass for you. He has a history from here that he would not wish to share with the American authorities. I am sure I could persuade him to help us."

Perhaps I could pay a visit to that L.A. neighbourhood when I'm finished in Nevada, thought Yousef.

"I will ask the T.V. people in London how much they will give us," said Mohammed, now in a rather down-trodden voice. "I know there is already over sixty thousand euros in our, 'Feed Syrian children' account in Gibraltar but we may still need it for something else."

CHAPTER 4

Julia Mackenzie or Jools as Alistair called her was, according to her family, the most accomplished woman in all of Bergen County. Juggling a career as a realtor, running a home, being a great mom and supporting her husband in his career were all part of her normal way of life. It was, however, not always this way after the sudden death of her first husband from a brain aneurism at the age of 22 while playing professional soccer in front of a crowd of sixteen thousand and one....Jools

Her world had fallen apart.

Meeting a slim, soft spoken, amiable big Scotsman looking for a home to rent in Dearborn a few years later was the start of her journey home. It was a journey to New Jersey and with a couple of great sons who looked like her husband and extolled 'old world' courtesy just like him.

Jools Mackenzie ran her business from the upper part of an old fire station in the county town of Elisabeth. The location wasn't ideal but it did have the advantage of a big population of over 100,000. There was also good parking, both for clients who wanted to drop in and also for Alistair, who could leave his car there and catch a train into the city. It took about an hour to get to Jool's office pushing and shoving along the Garden state parkway, but with the boys old enough to travel on the school bus and have keys for the house it avoided Alistair taking a car into New York City and gave the couple a valuable hour together most mornings. Jools usually kept her black Porsche 911 Carerra Targa in one of the two big garages she rented beside her office. The car had a dual purpose both to impress the clients and to give her transport home if Alistair was working later than her or travelling overnight.

Yes, she had done well for herself but not without losing some of the gentleness and soft manners of the girl she used to be before her first tragic loss. The song says, 'what doesn't kill us makes us stronger,' and this was Jools Mackenzie in a nutshell.

"Hi Bernice, its Jools. Is Alistair in the office still? Oh, right, a planning meeting. I just wondered when he would be coming home because I have a really big potential listing here in Elisabeth and the only time they can see me is at 7.00 this evening. Yeah, the kids will be fine. I just phoned them. Ok, well, would you tell him to look at his emails when he comes out and if he can get a lift home from one of the guys just to take it? Yes, I think he still has his pilot's licence up to date. In fact I'm sure of it. That's a shame, but if Alistair has to hire a plane then he won't mind. He loves flying, especially if he gets to try out something new, even better if it's at the company's expense. Yes, I would just go ahead and book it if it's the only way he can get to the last launch at Carson City. I'll just be glad when he's home. What with George leaving and all, it's going to be a hell of a week all round."

Bernice put the finishing touches to her bosses plan. All the dates and some of the hotels booked for George were going to be the same, just needing a change of name, but the direction Alistair was starting from was different as was his return trip. Also, a demonstrator car and a driver would need to be arranged for some parts of the journey along with a return flight to New York. And then there was Montgomerie Ford in Carson City. 'Big' Jim Montgomerie junior was the unofficial leader for the area's Dealer Committee. Alistair could not afford to alienate him because he would be the loudest voice on some of the tougher changes to the franchise agreement that were coming as a package, along with the new models being launched across the year. Upsetting Jim might build more of an uphill struggle. But how to get Alistair to Carson City on time? There was no scheduled or even chartered aircraft that flew the route Alistair needed. Thankfully the Internet provided what looked like an answer. Nordstrom modern aircraft hire (We fly the best in the West) operating on a private airstrip some 185 miles North East of Carson City, might fill the time gap and keep 'Big Jim' quiet for once. Hiring a small plane might seem a bit dramatic, but Jools seemed to think Alistair would approve and Bernice had worked with him long enough to know that talking to one was like talking to them both. They tended to agree on almost everything.

"Jed Nordstrom, yeah, we can fly to Carson City. Sure… we can do it on that day. Single engine, American built Beech. Latest model with a very high spec. Specially ordered for the famous diversified conditions we enjoy in these parts, you understand. Well sure… he can fly it himself but we would need an awful lot of insurance on a new aircraft like that. I don't need a deposit but if you could give me a run through of a meaty enough credit card we'll get everything waiting for him. I do that route all the time. I'm happy to take him. How's he going to get here? By car you say and he will want to come back to his vehicle that same evening. So will you want me to store his vehicle here? I can do that. We can park it in our hanger locked up safe. Tell me if there are any last minute changes otherwise just send him on up. No, just tell him to ask for me personally when he gets here. I'll be in the little office out back or in the hangar. Remember, 'we fly the best in the west.'

CHAPTER 5

It was different for Mohammed. Unlike Yousef and all the other foreign fighters, he was born and brought up in Syria. He remembered it from before the war and, when he managed to sleep, which was not that often now, he even dreamed about it.

His favourite dream took him back to his parent's house near the busy market on the outskirts of Aleppo. It did not seem to matter to Mohammed how many places he had lived in since, the house in his dreams was always the one he grew up in and always Mustafa, his youngest brother, was there playing in and out of the dream. Not with a horribly disfigured face like on the day Mohammed carried his lifeless body home after his junior school was bombed by government jets. No, Mustafa was always the beautiful little boy with brown curly hair and a permanent smile on his face that Mohammed's troubled mind would love to see, just one more time.

Mohammed did not know if Yousef had any family or what his deepest reasons for coming to fight were. He knew that Yousef was admired by the leaders for his religious devotion and especially because he would use a knife, something the others spoke of often, but were rarely able to carry out themselves.

Mohammed's reasons for taking part in the war were personal. They lay in a deep rooted desire to avenge the loss of his brother, the destruction of his parents' home and that damage turning his father and mother into refugees instead of retirees, which had long been their plan. Mohammed appreciated all the help his cause had received from people coming to join in the fight for justice and revenge. However, he wondered if any of them could really know what it felt to have the blood of their family staining their memories for all time, as he did.

For a brief moment Mohammed allowed himself to day dream about a Syria reborn. A Syria that was a place of happiness and safety that praised God and respected sharia law; where women were obedient to their husbands and fathers, and their sons studied the Quran. If he could help bring that about then all the blood and sacrifice and the horrors he had witnessed would have been worthwhile. Right now he had work to do and he would not tire until it was done.

Mohammed had hidden the journalist's Toyota Land Cruiser in an underground car park next to the Baron Hotel in Aleppo. He had briefly worked there in the reception, as a young man, and had many happy memories of the elegant hotel and its often famous international guests. The list included Agatha Christie, who, many decades before, wrote the first part of one of her most famous stories, 'Murder on the Orient Express', while a resident there. Syria was a good place to live back then and had remained so until quite recently. Just how it had become the living hell he now knew, Mohammed could no longer remember. Although, he thought, his country's descent into the abyss, mirrored his own passage from a respected brother and much loved son to a man with nowhere on this earth to return to and not even a place he could safely call home. He had become the loneliest kind of gipsy with only God to provide solace and an ice cold fear of Yousef to keep him from trying to find some way back.

Standing with one foot on the front, bumper-mounted, power take off, 8500 lb winch, he lifted the heavy hood of the Toyota and pushed an old metal table leg under it to keep it propped up. When he last saw the car Mohammed had removed the number plates, any identifying stickers, the tracker, hidden in what Mohammed thought was an obvious spot in the passenger front foot well, and he'd taken out the battery, before leaving the 4X4 cocooned behind a few old interior doors and a dusty, dark blue sheet. The car was exactly as he had left it, near to the entrance of the dark abandoned car park. At one time there was an abundance of cars to be had for the price of a few rounds fired in the air. But now good cars were becoming harder to find and good tyres were almost impossible. He had kept the Land Cruiser mainly because of its brand new set of Michelin X series, sand and gravel tyres, which would enable it to leave the road and travel even on the hot shifting sand that had caught out so many frightened, fleeing city dwellers, only a couple of years before, with their sedan cars full of relatives and roof racks full of memories.

After connecting the battery, the dash lit up brightly and with only one turn of the key, the big six cylinder diesel coughed its way back to life in typical Toyota fashion. The brakes were another issue. Mohammed pushed the car into first and reverse repeatedly until the seized back brakes finally and suddenly freed and the big car lurched forward, narrowly missing a solid concrete pillar.

On a wide screen deep in the heart of 'Doughnut', the staff's name for the operational headquarters for GCHQ in Cheltenham, a small triangle trailing the code F564/9 appeared and began to flash.

Moments later an encrypted signal about F564/9 was passed to CIA Langley having been dictated by The Deputy Director section 12 C (Syrian conflict zone) and approved by Rob H. the Director General.

The message read:

Highest Priority. Back up tracker device fitted to Jeep of kidnapped France 24 journalist, Schneider and party, recommenced signalling at 12.43 GMT today. We have a current location of: 36,2050 Degrees North and 15,000 Degrees East. Placing it at Baron Street, Aleppo Syria.

Our D.G. askes if you could please get a drone on it (priority 1) and pass the images to our screens here at GCHQ. Authorisation code: ARH/UKR/90765C

After waiting until it was dark, Mohammed drove the big Land Cruiser along the carefully planned route through the narrow streets to the abandoned bakery that had become his headquarters in the previous few hours. Every obstacle, sniper and known I.E.D had to be carefully manoeuvred around with width and distance considered to the inch to avoid disaster. Mohammed liked to drive fast but not on this trip. He was blissfully unaware of his silent companion. A US Navy drone hung in the air high above him. It was picking up a heat signal from the engine, a radar signal from the steel bodywork, a heat signal from Mohammed himself and a transmission from the back-up tracker well hidden in the headlining. Powered by the cable attached to the central cabin light, it was also revealing his position to the drone operator thousands of miles away.

The Habib bakery had survived almost untouched as it served all sides in the war and for a long time was out of bounds for most fighters who used women and children to pay for and collect bread. Only the lack of flour and water and the credible threat from Yousef to crucify the elderly baker in front of his family caused the two sons and the old man to beg free passage and make a run for it, leaving behind a small, solid, steel-reinforced concrete, flat-roofed building, containing no bread, a little flour, mostly spread across the floor and a single lemon tree, now missing it's lemons, in the kidney shaped small garden at the back.

CHAPTER 6

Jools loved her home. In fact the desire to own a really impressive house in a great neighbourhood was what prompted her to go into real estate all those years ago. Most of the furnishings were to her taste, American colonial to match the exterior of her classic house. Alistair and Jools did not always share each other's ideas when it came to décor and furnishing. She could just about cope with Alistair's father's family's influence, all broad swords and shields. Alistair's mother was Persian and because of this his den had many quirky eastern references and smells including the colourful rugs, huge cushions, large metal lanterns and the tall shisha standing in the corner. She really did miss him when he was away from home. Hell, she would even let him light the shisha just to have him around.

Jools walked through the kitchen and passed the gloss-white, ornately carved, internal door connecting the kitchen to the wide, brightly illuminated, five car garage. She stopped for a moment and ran her hand along the fender of her husband's prized possession, his pale green metallic, 1970's Lincoln Continental coupe. Growing up in Scotland, Alistair had been introduced to the USA through an early push-button colour television. Shows like Bonanza and Colombo had brought entertainment to an almost perpetual greyness in his comfortable red-sandstone home. This greyness and the time spent in his home were caused mainly by the wet and windy weather of the West of Scotland. However, it was always the T.V. shows with automobiles in them that really took the interest of the young, car mad boy. Kojac, Streets of San Francisco and best of all, Cannon, featuring a shiny new Lincoln Continental coupe driven by a short, fat, balding detective, were sure fire favourites. He always said to himself, 'If that guy can get a car like that, so can I,' and here was over eighteen feet, from hood ornament to continental spare wheel kit, of living proof, polished and attached to a battery charger in the centre of their garage.

It's a bit too early to phone Alistair, Jools thought as she settled into her favourite arm chair, beside the baby grand piano, in front of her sixty inch, curved TV, in their music room."

***

"In CNN World report tonight we look at the reasons why thousands of young Muslim men are leaving their homes in Europe and heading for the Middle East to become fighters. What impact will their return have on our homeland security? Our special correspondent, Peter Steel, is in Belfast and sends this report.

"I'm joined today in the studio by Mrs. Brenda McConnell who is the mother of eight, grown-up children. One of her sons, Daniel, became one of the first young British Muslims to go abroad seeking Jihad.

"Mrs McConnell."

"Oh please, call me Brenda."

"Brenda, have you heard from your son recently?"

"No, not for several years."

"Now, this is a photograph of him taken a long time ago."

"Yes, that's my Daniel; he calls himself Yousef these days."

"This programme is beamed all over the world. If he is watching, do you have a message for him?"

"Come home, Dan. Your sister Mary is very ill in the Belfast City hospital. It's the same thing that took your uncle, when you were little. Mary has been asking for you.

"Dan was always Mary's favourite brother and she desperately needs him now; she's very ill in the oncology unit and he'll really need to hurry if he's going to get home for her."

"How did he become interested in Jihad?"

"After he converted from our faith, he spent hours in his room watching videos that a visiting Imam was sending to him."

"Do you think he might return?"

"I don't think so, but I pray for him to see sense and come back to his home and our family. We don't care what you've done; come back and we'll all be here for you. Your brother Paul is a lawyer now and he says he can help you."

**

Jools stared at the big screen like she was looking at a ghost. The clarity and detail of the big, ultra-high definition T.V. was impressive and the photograph put up by CNN of a tall, slim, dark haired, blue-eyed, young man in his early twenties wearing a Rugby shirt and chinos, could easily have been taken of her husband Alistair at the same age. His hair was a little different, but there was no mistaking the bone structure and build of this look alike, even the way he stood.

Jools thought about the possibilities and realised she should tell Alistair. It was hard enough to get through airport security and keep to his back-breaking schedule without the added problem of looking like a now well publicised terrorist. That's all he needs, she thought as she reached for her mobile phone and tried to get hold of her husband.

CHAPTER 7

Due east of Miller's Mountain lies the small town of Molinos Ridge. The locals have come to believe that the town, and some say, America, has more of a past than a future. The local industry consisted of a large, single, chemical factory, long since closed. Only the abandoned buildings and the slight sulphur smell hanging over the old factory, hold one answer to the question, 'why do so many of the townsfolk look so old?'

One of the very few younger people you were likely to meet in Molinos Ridge was Sheriff Carlton Culzean.

Carlton, a well-educated young man had, in his spare time, compared the demographics of Molinos Ridge to that of a similar size of town in rural Japan. Funny, he thought, that the old Japs and some of our old guys' parents once slugged it out with each other in a war and now none of them has anyone to pass their homes, farms and businesses on to.

Carlton's father held the job of Sheriff before him. His father died a couple of years earlier and out of respect Carlton always wore his late father's pearl handled, special order, long barrel Colt 45 as his 'on duty' sidearm. Carlton's younger sister Rose, when not disappearing off to spend time with her boyfriend Roy, the local doctor, was his deputy. Molinos Ridge was in many ways a typical western town with all the action rippling out from the main street. On one side of the street, the biggest landmark was the only four storey building in town. The Union Hotel with eighteen letting bedrooms and a quite decent restaurant below, had a furnished ground floor terrace for people to down a beer or two in the fresh pine scented mountain air that settled on the town especially during the warm summer nights. The Union was also one of the few places in town where you could get Wi-Fi and a reasonable cell phone signal as all the local masts protruded from the water tank on top of the building's wide, flat roof. Beside the hotel was a big scale, cement built parking lot, laid out in large blocks like the runway of an old aerodrome, big enough for over one hundred and fifty cars. The lot was transformed once a year for the Molinos Ridge mountain bike festival that saw competitors from all over the USA arrive in camper vans and very briefly put the place on the map, before allowing it to return to obscurity again just three days later.

Carlton's office, twice the size now needed for the shrinking community, was built in the art-deco, liner style, popular in the 1930's and sat proudly, if a bit shabbily, atop fifty, broad white steps directly across the main street from the oversized parking lot. Built long before the idea of wheelchair access was even thought of, an out of place dark grey GRP ramp with an orange painted, steel balustrade ran uncomfortably down the side of the wide steps to a single, orange painted, designated disabled parking space in the road below. The 'disabled only' sign had two large bullet holes in it and a dent in the pole where someone had reversed into it while trying to park.

Placed recently on a lamppost at the front entrance to the Union Hotel hung a public notice. It was held on with a piece of string and printed on one side of a piece of pink paper then carefully wrapped in a plastic pocket for protection.

ATTENTION ALL RESIDENTS OF MOLINOS RIDGE.

*There will be a public meeting at the UNION HOTEL Wednesday (14th) at 18.30 hours to discuss the proposals of **Anglo American Shale Oil** to carry out Fracturing for Natural Gas in and around our Town.*

Representatives of Anglo American Shale Oil will be in attendance to answer your questions. No dogs or guns allowed on the night. Refreshments provided.

-

Carlton put another piece of his favourite cinnamon chewing gum in his mouth and looked carefully at the sign.

"How do they know there is any gas here?" asked Rose, tilting her head and sweeping her long dyed blonde hair back to reveal a perplexed look in her small but bright, hazel eyes. Rose had come to believe that Carlton knew the answer to almost everything and Carlton rarely disappointed her.

"Do you remember last year, there were those two geologists with the big silver pick up, staying at the Union Hotel for over a month?"

"Yes, I especially remember the small good looking one. I told him he had a nice shovel."

"Oh yeah, I remember that well; the fat guy with him turned out to be his boyfriend. The look on your face when you found out! Some detective you turned out to be."

"Yeah, well, he didn't exactly wave a rainbow flag or anything and you know what they say. Them that doesn't ask doesn't get."

"Well, we both know all that you'd have got from him, don't we?"

"A card at Christmas?"

"Exactly."

"Anyway, locating a gas field. The two gay guys sent a couple of crates of rock samples down to their lab in Austen, Texas, and the next group who turned up in the Union Hotel were the seismologists, who kept half the pensioners in town awake in the afternoon with compressors, explosions and that big thumper machine."

Rose's eyes opened wide. "I remember all the calls we got about that. Old Bob was going out to stop them with his antique, Winchester rifle, till you stopped him."

"I could have saved those oil men a lot of trouble. For a big fee I could have rented them my dog. There isn't anything God or man has made that he couldn't sniff out including Natural Gas."

"I guess so."

"Do you think many will come to this meeting?"

"It will be standing room only. It doesn't take a sniffer dog to sniff out the money a few people can make from this."

"And the others?"

"That's where your protesters are going to come from. Anyone who misses out on the money will be going green."

"You mean environmentalists."

"No Rose, I mean green with envy! A poor town like this needs a few new, flashy rich folk like we need another parking lot on a week day afternoon. Anyway just be sure you are available here a good half an hour before the meeting. We might just have to deal with what passes for a riot, here in Molinos Ridge."

CHAPTER 8

Achmed opened the white, security tagged envelope in his own small sitting room. It was situated above the garage and the machine room which contained the ride on mower for the gardens of the mansion house of his millionaire employer. He didn't want his boss, or anyone else, to see his 'replacement' U.S. passport that he'd organised especially to send out to his cousin Mohammed for Yousef to use to illegally enter the U.S.A.

Achmed removed the folded paper list of chocolates from the red, heart shaped box and, slipped the passport in between a brightly coloured birthday card. Then he placed the card in the box and wrapped the whole thing in gold and black striped, fancy metallic, wrapping paper. Using Scotch tape to seal it up, including the corners, he then put on the label with its Lebanon address on the front and a fictitious name and address on the back as the sender.

He smiled at the sender address. 'There can't be many people sending chocolates to terrorists from a 90210 zip code. Just as long as it goes through the post office X ray machines without being opened. I will have done as Mohammed asked and he will not tell anyone what he knows about me. If the passport does get found, I can say I lost the last one and I lost this one too. I'm very absent minded with documents and things. Yes, that's what I could say.'Achmed thought.

***

The blood ran down Mohammed's arm as the old rope used to hang him by his wrists from the ceiling of the bakery cut into him. He had wet himself and his legs were beginning to itch in the heat. A mixture of piss, blood and flour made a strange pattern across his left, grey coloured, Nike shoe. The right one lay on the floor where Yousef had dragged him to the ceiling hook formerly used to hang bags of flour.

"You lied to me," screamed Yousef. "You wanted this passport for yourself! It doesn't look like me, it looks like you! What was I going to do at Kennedy airport? Tell them I'd shrunk three inches and grown a new face?

"First my stupid mother betrays me on television and now you. Tell me you got this passport for yourself and I might deal leniently with you. If you lie to me again I'll finish you like a dog."

"It was just a mistake," begged Mohammed. "I had not seen him without a beard since he was young. His eyes are the same colour. I'm really sorry."

"This has cost me a lot of time. Our enemies are closing in on us."

Yousef looked at his recently acquired watch. "4.30, we'd better get moving."

Using the eight inch blade kept in a sheath attached to his belt, he cut the rope holding Mohammed

33

aloft and Mohammed fell onto his knees. All this drama came as no surprise to anyone. Yousef's mood could change in an instant and he seemed to need a few moments of eruption every day just to clear his mind.

"You take this, you might need it," said Yousef as he dropped Achmed's passport into Mohammad's open backpack.

After a couple of hours had elapsed, Yousef stood up straight looking at a blank wall with his back to Mohammed. "How are the other travel arrangements for me to go to America?" he asked, in his normal calm and less irritated voice.

Mohammed thought carefully before answering. "Our friends in London have provided all the currency we will need. Tickets have been purchased for every leg of the journey except the last one from Dublin to JFK. I have the Land Cruiser fuelled up and nearby so we can leave this place."

"Have you checked the Land cruiser for trackers?"

"Yes, I found the tracker and removed it. Also the stickers on the sides and the roof are now gone and I found some number plates from a shot up car and screwed them on. I have set up the sat-nav and put maps in the car just in case.

"We have bribed the Kurds who are in charge outside Afrin to take you across the border. You will have to shave your beard and cut your hair to become Irish once again. Your cover story is that you are a journalist with Sky news. I kept the body armour with press written on it which we took off Schneider to complete the story. After that we have a change of plan."

"What change of plan?" growled Yousef.

"You will be taken to the small Turkish sea port of Silifke where you will board a sailing yacht that will bring you to Lamaka marina in Cyprus. Lamaka is a local marina, but also an official customs entry point. We have paid a substantial bribe to the officials and they are waiting to welcome you. They even have a suitcase of Marks and Spencer clothes in your size, sent from our friends in London, waiting in the Harbour Masters office. From there you will board a holiday flight straight to Dublin. Our Irish republican friends have a room for you at the Radisson Blu on the airport campus. I have asked them and they have just agreed to get an Irish passport for you. It will be left in the hotel by a room service attendant."

"Now that's what I call room service," Yousef said, with the first smile all day returning to his face.

"And the other passports, passes, cash, credit cards?"

"All in the glove box of the car."

"Good, light a fire with lots of smoke so it looks like we're still here. We'll leave in one hour."

CHAPTER 9

Alistair had a secret. It was eleven o 'clock in the morning and his plane did not leave until seven. Ample time to visit Felice, he thought. He carefully took out the worn piece of paper from his wallet and ran his finger down the list of 'fake' phone numbers until he reached the only real one on the small, hand written sheet.

"Hi Felice, it's Alistair. Can I see you today? Yes, in an hour. You can? Twelve thirty will be fine. Yeah, I'll call you when I'm outside and you can buzz me in."

Felice had told him that if you want to know a man's secrets then there are three places to look where you would be sure to discover the truth. One was in his phone, another was the trunk of his car and lastly in his garage. Alistair took heed of this advice. If there was one person in New York who knew about men and their secrets it was Felice. He always deleted any calls to or from Felice, kept her number written down but hidden. His car trunk was quite empty apart from carrier bags and boxes of Ford literature and his garage was filled with cars, garden tools and empty suitcases in a variety of sizes. Therefore nothing was there that could lead Jools or anyone else to his most private secret.

In the bottom drawer of his filing cabinet he kept a green box file marked 'Obsolete Models'. In this file Alistair kept a couple of old CD's and an empty matchbox and inside that were three packets of four Viagra tablets. Alistair looked at his watch and at eleven-thirty precisely swallowed one of the blue, diamond shaped tablets before carefully returning the remaining ones to the matchbox and placing the matchbox back in the file.

On the ground floor Alistair headed to the wall of cash machines. He quickly looked in his wallet, $180 in notes. The first two machines said, 'NOT IN SERVICE' and Alistair became a little agitated at the prospect of having to wander about looking for a machine that worked, especially with Felice's appointment already booked and his Viagra coming to the boil just in time for his secret encounter. Third time lucky, thought Alistair as he withdrew three hundred dollars and put Felice's two hundred and fifty dollar fee in the back part of the wallet. The remaining fifty joined his other cash in the front section.

As Alistair sat in the back of the yellow cab his Samsung Galaxy cell phone gave the familiar melodic whistle that told him he had received an SMS message. 'Come early if you want. Felice. XXX'. It was 12.15 and Alistair raced up the thirteen steps to the front of the traditional brownstone building and pressed the top buzzer, the buzzer bearing no name. The door almost immediately clicked, unlocked and sprang forward half an inch. As he entered the large, darkened hall a single LED bulb, attached to a long flex suspended from the high ceiling above him, flashed into light. Felice's large, expensive apartment was on the top floor. He moved swiftly up the stairs, all the time hoping to avoid any of the other residents who might choose that precise moment to leave their apartment and perhaps talk to him. As he reached the top apartment he saw the double doors had been opened. Felice's head peaked round the door and she beckoned him in.

She stood before him in a light blue, silk robe. Only the patent black, 'super-high' heels and black stockings which were showing beneath, giving an indication of what an appointment with her was all about, and what Alistair was going to get during his $250 hour-long session. Felice was French and greeted him in what Alistair had come to believe was the sexiest accent he knew.

"Ah, Alis-tair, ow ar yu?" She closed the big, mahogany and stained glass door with her left hand. She pulled him by the cuff of his jacket towards her and kissed him slowly on the lips. Alistair's hands ran down her back and squeezed her buttocks like he was squeezing a perfect piece of firm summer fruit.

Everything about the bedroom was now very familiar to him. Alistair took off his jacket and hung it on the ornate metal hook behind the bedroom door. He then took off his expensive Florsheim Imperial, Kenmoor brogue shoes that Mr. Ford himself had recommended he buy, when Alistair admired them at the company's Presidents award gala last fall. If they're good enough for the head of the company, they're good enough for me, he thought while he watched Felice undress. As she slipped out of her silk robe, she answered one of her three phones accepting an appointment for 2pm.

In front of him was the king size bed with no headboard, but lots of extra pillows. A large, colourful beach towel lay flat across the bedspread on the centre of the bed. There was an oak bedside cabinet with an old fashioned, glass-type air freshener on it. The black metal T.V. stand held a forty inch, flat screen T.V.and a C.D. player with fifty C.D's stored below. Alistair began to fold his clothes as he took them off, placing them on a gilded, Louis XV chair. Immediately above the bed were ten mirror tiles set as one, large, single mirror. This reflected against the mirror tiles on the wall behind the bed. In the ceiling, near the bedroom door, an antique-style wooden fan kept the whole room cool if a bit noisy.

As Alistair undressed another of Felice's cell phones rang and she answered it.

"I'm sorree, I'm beesse. Call me when you get eere. But don't call me for at least an hour. Au revoir, Monsieur."

As she ended her call Alistair's eyes took in the curve of her body and the neat little inch gap of shaved gold hair between the tops of her legs.

"I am very beesse just now," explained Felice, as she came over and stood behind Alistair with the cell phone in her right hand, sending a text while running her left hand slowly and expertly up and down his now aroused manhood. In the corner Alistair saw her riding crop and black, knee-high leather boots. Felice genuinely loved sex, especially when she was in charge. She had turned a hobby, some might say an obsession, into a very successful cash business. However, Alistair wasn't interested in being dominated. He actually shared Felice's preference for being in charge in the bedroom. It added to his excitement that Felice spent all day and part of the night getting guys to perform for her, beating them with a stick or riding them with a strap-on and here he was taking complete control of her and making her obey his words and actions.

She had never failed to get him to come, even when his mind was elsewhere or when he was unwell or exhausted. Today was no exception and for a few moments he forgot everything as he gave in to a momentary feeling of complete pleasure followed by some very heavy breathing while they held each other tight.

After sex, Felice asked Alistair to lie face down on the bed while she squirted body cream on his back. She kept the cream in a fridge and was delighted that it made him shudder as it hit his body.

"Have you been naughty?" she asked as she pinched his neck before returning to softly massaging his back.

"No, but I bet you have," he laughed as he

turned around and squeezed her right breast pulling the back of her head with his other hand so her lips were pushed firmly onto his.

When the session came to an end, Alistair took his gold, Rolex Oyster watch, an anniversary gift from Jools, out of his shoe and placed it on his right wrist. He dressed first before paying Felice. He always dressed fast, because his interest in sex had been fully satisfied and because he didn't want to be caught there undressed if something should happen.

As he was leaving, Felice offered him a luxury Belgian chocolate from a silver tray she kept near the apartment's front door.

"One of my other clee-ents gave me this. I don't eat a lot as you know, but please remember to bring me some pens from your office next time. I am always needing pens."

Alistair headed down the stairs and checked his emails on the smartphone before checking his voicemail.

"Hi Alistair; you asked me to remind you to get toothpaste at the airport, as the one in your bathroom had run dry this morning. Have a safe flight, Darling. I'll call you tonight when you land in L.A."

"Not the only thing of mine that's now run dry," he thought wryly as he hailed another yellow cab.

As Alistair sped across the City back to his office, he wondered which part of his background had given him both the occasional need for sex in the afternoon and also the ability to be totally detached from it emotionally, after the event. He thought being a Glasgow boy gave him a really honest view of himself. Having his balls professionally emptied was to him just like going for a haircut at the barbers. He didn't want to be in front of people with long unmanaged hair and he didn't want to be going around with full, unmanaged balls. Or maybe it was the Iranian part of his heritage from his mother's side. Some of his ancestors must have enjoyed having a harem. His mind was filled with the smell of frankincense and the sounds of Arabic music that must have played in the woman's section of an imagined ancestor's palace. He decided to save that thought for his next shower when he was at the hotel across from his first Dealer launch the following morning.

***

Big Jim was on the warpath. He might have had the Carson City Ford dealership in the family for two generations, but not since the launch of the ill-fated Edsel in his granddad's time, in the late nineteen fifties, had a Company Vice President agreed to come to one of his model launches. Even though there was 36 hours to go, Jim was going to make sure everything ran smoothly.

"No, I told you before, I want to taste all the food before you serve it to my customers and especially Mr. Mackenzie. Have you found out what the Mackenzie motto is yet? Yep, I already know it's Scottish, but what does it mean in American English. I need to know it so I can impress him that even out here we have acquired SOME culture.

"I shine – not burn. What in hell's name does that mean? Well this showroom and car lot had better shine or you'll burn, think on that!"

Almost all the staff had learned to stay out of Big Jim's way when he was in this type of mood. One of the sales guys had devised a colour chart for his neck, starting at white and passing through pink before reaching fire truck red, with a variety of comments listed below with only one word shown under the deepest red. RUN!

Almost despite Big Jim's efforts to push people around, a 'by the book' dealer launch was starting to take shape. All the flag stands that were secured by placing them under the offside front wheel of the cars, at the front of the lot, were now in place to greet visitors. The window graphics were carefully pressed into the edges of the big showroom windows.

"No bubbles," shouted Jim.

Three demonstrator cars in patriotic red, white and metallic blue sat under the sign. 'Drive a deal today' and the local radio personality had been emailed his script for the night of the launch. The three showroom cars were in the preparation shop awaiting polish and detailing and the sales team had been issued crib sheets on the new specification and prices.

"Don't give them out just yet," warned Jim and each sales person had been assigned their own list of expected visitors to target. Jim had been told that despite the fact that Alistair was delighted with the offer to spend the night at his ranch, he was going to fly in and out on the same day to try and maintain his tight schedule. Because Alistair had added the footnote, 'and my wife is expecting me home after a week of unexpected travelling,' Jim was happy not to see it as any sort of slight, but instead, just another New Yorker under his wife's thumb.

Still to come was the roulette tables with the imitation money, the race night stand and the national, 'Win the new car' competition banner and the draw tickets. Jim had already phoned the trucking company twice and had been assured that everything was where it should be at that time.

Across the network all the dealerships were reaching the same stage of preparedness just as Alistair had gone through his own rituals and preparations to travel and perform in front of customers, the buying public and local (often very local) news media.

CHAPTER 10

For such a big car the lack of legroom at the front of the Land Cruiser made long legged Yousef uncomfortable. He preferred to fold down the back bench seat and lie on a couple of gold velour sofa backrests taken from the abandoned apartment they had 'liberated' from the baker's family. On this comfortable surface Yousef was able to get some sleep while Mohammed drove them through the night to their meeting point close to the north western border.

Deep in the Pentagon building, behind a steel security door marked 'U.A.V. front line command, section 12', Corporal Bill H. Bradley sat in front of a wide bank of three screens. They controlled a mark three Predator drone armed with two Hellfire 'L' type guided missiles and the latest radar satellite positioning system for the U.A.V. or unmanned aerial vehicle. The drone was equipped with a General Electric 'phoebe' laser guidance system for the missiles.

"Target continues north-west towards A-Zaz. There are two people on board. I think the passenger may be held captive in the back of the vehicle. He is lying down in the back and has not moved for a while. There is a feint heat signal from him, so he is alive but might be drugged."

A voice in Bill's headphones crackled, "O.K. continue to monitor. Let me know if there are any changes and make sure you are ready to fire on my signal without delay."

Bill checked the missile arming systems and locked onto the Toyota both in readiness and as a systems check. Everything came up with a green light on his screens.

In the distance Mohammed could see a makeshift roadblock, consisting of two old pick-up trucks with heavy machine guns mounted on their roofs parked at right angles to each other with the machine guns unmanned and pointing to the sky.

"Wake up, Yousef, I think it's them."

Yousef sat bolt upright, picked up his AK47 and held it close to his side.

"Drive slowly and stop about fifty meters from them. Then stick both your hands in the air, and let them come to us." Mohammed did as he was told.

Two heavily armed men in dusty stained and ripped uniforms approached the driver's window.

"Are you the one who wants to cross the border?" They pointed to Yousef.

Mohamed answered, "Are you the sons of Ben Ali?"

They did not answer him but instead asked, "Have you the money our father asked for?"

Yousef pulled open a plastic carrier bag and showed the contents. One of the two men, without speaking, leaned into the car and took the bag and immediately walked away and placed it onto the front bench seat of the nearest of the two pick-up trucks.

Yousef opened his back-pack and looked at his highly valued, full roll of Italian 'Tenderly' brand toilet paper he had found on the back floor of the Toyota. It must have belonged to Aldo the photographer. "Well, I wiped him out, and now I can have a wipe on him," he joked to himself holding the toilet roll up like a trophy.

"I'm going for a dump," he told Mohammed. "Why don't you invite our new friends into our car to enjoy a drink of water with our air conditioning on and I'll join you when I'm finished."

Yousef picked up his back-pack and walked down an incline about sixty meters to a large rock that he could lean against and empty his bowels.

Bill H. Bradley gave his report in his most urgent voice. "The Toyota has come to a halt in front of two armed vehicles. They have let the captive leave the Toyota, I believe, to perform a call of nature. He is carrying a toilet roll. All three combatants are now in the Toyota. The captive is wearing the word 'PRESS' on his clothing and he is possibly Aldo Morretti the missing Italian photographer.

"Is the captive clear of the impact area?"

"Affirmative," said Bill.

"Authority to proceed at 11.47 Hours: P.T."

The explosion caused by two hellfire missiles hitting a Toyota Land Cruiser with forty five litres of diesel fuel in its tank blew Yousef face forward into the sand and he almost fell unconscious from the sudden loss of oxygen caused by the vacuum effect. I'm glad I had a dump first or I would need a new set of pants as well as a new assistant, he thought as he rose to his feet to look at the damage. There was not one part of the Toyota left that was bigger than one foot long, and a deep, blackened crater stood where two tons of vehicle was ticking over only moments earlier. Fortunately, both the pickup trucks were still intact and the one with the bag of money in it also had the keys sitting in the ignition. Yousef dropped to his knees in prayer at the side of the road and thanked Allah for his deliverance. This was truly a sign that he had divine help on his mission.

Yousef thought about the position he found himself in. He stroked his chin ready to run his hand through his beard only to find a few hours of stubble, having shaved earlier for the first time in months. Well here I am, a British Citizen with a bag full of money, a reporter's outfit, a whole load of identity documents and transport. And those silly bastards think they just killed me! It doesn't get a lot better than this, he thought as he jumped into the pick-up, opened the map and looked through the now cracked windscreen, before pointing the car towards the border. Yousef thought that being a journalist was a pretty good cover. Despite being given a hard time at school for his poor reading and writing, Yousef thought he had a way with words. In any case journalists would often travel around Groom Lake sending 'alien' reports from Area 51 and therefore he would draw very little attention from locals and the police.

**

The journey to JFK was always an annoying one. Heavy traffic and grumpy cab drivers usually made it a time to sit using his laptop or consult his smartphone.

Alistair's driver had recently returned to NYC from Iran and Alistair delighted in discussing his mother's family home and breaking into some of the Farsi he learned from his mother and uncles as a child. This made the journey seem much quicker and he felt well as he headed for his long flight.

Ford had an account with, and therefore a preference to use, United Airlines. The premier access service for first class passengers got Alistair through the airport efficiently, and he even had time for a complimentary Hendricks Gin and tonic with crushed ice and a slice of lime before settling in to his oversized, charcoal leather, reclining seat in the reserved forward section of the wide-bodied plane.

Of all the perks that went with a big job in a big company, the stratospheric limit on his company credit card was the best, he thought. However, there were a few limits recently imposed on how he could use it. A few years ago he might have been able to put Felice down as a legitimate expense under therapeutic massage or something similar. All that came to an end following stories circulating round the financial auditors. It was reputed that a high flying executive in a supplier company put an almost $5,000 visit to a lap dance joint in London down as 'Lap top repairs'. The story goes he was only found out when his lap top broke down the following week and I.T. could find no warranty on the repairs. True or not, some rules came into force for Vice Presidents like Alistair for the very first time.

Still, he thought, when you are on a red eye, it's nice to get a seat you can sleep in and some blankets to give you the illusion you're home in bed. The 19.00 flight from JFK to LAX was certainly a red eye. At six hours and twenty-five minutes it was always going to be a strain, and due to the time difference he would land (if there were no delays) at 22.25 hours local time. At least the time difference meant he would get some sleep at the Woodland Hills Marriot before needing to get ready for the first launch of the trip at Woodland Lincoln Ford.

Since the decision to phase out the Mercury brand was taken, the idea of producing a special coupe carrying the Mercury name was always going to appeal to brand purists. The super modern styling, reminiscent of a Rolls Royce Wraith, would have instant showroom appeal as well. Thanks to the unusual dual colour combinations, and twenty-two inch, alloy wheels, this limited edition was bound to be an instant classic and hopefully keep the dealers happy while their mainstream model franchise agreement was being softened in the direction of the manufacturer.

Every first class passenger had access to United Airlines Directv service. Alistair looked to find the report that Jools had told him about, the one with his doppelganger in it.

"Can I get you anything from the bar, Sir?"

Not bad, thought Alistair. Nice ass, shame about the oversize chest, it makes her look a bit cheap even though it's probably the most expensive thing on her.

"Could I have a large gin and tonic with ice and lemon?"

"Gordon's alright?"

"Yes, that will be fine."

Alistair almost spilled his drink when he looked at the image. Jools wasn't joking, he thought. The photo on his seventeen inch HD screen set into the backrest of the leather seat in front of him could actually be him. He listened intently as the gloomy little lady from Belfast told her sad tale of the good boy who had gone bad, then went away.

It was going to be a long night and an even longer day tomorrow so he would need to get some sleep if he was going to be worth a damn. Alistair pushed the silver toggle to adjust his chair into its fully reclined position. Using the remote, he turned off the screen and his reading light and settled into the soft, white pillow and complimentary dark blue blankets that the nameless girl with the nice ass had provided for him. He dreamed of another hour with Felice and a weekend at home with Jools, his two favourite New York ways to relax and recharge, as he slowly drifted into a deep, black sleep, devoid of cars, Irish Jihadists or franchise agreements.

***

In Belfast and across the United Kingdom the early editions of Britain's best -selling newspaper, the Sun, were arriving on newsstands and people's doorsteps. The headline on page one read….

IS THIS MAN JIHADI MICK?

His name is Daniel, brought up in a staunch Catholic family in Belfast. He was radicalised in his local mosque. His mother and family want him home. Could this be the black-robed jihadist who has butchered journalists and aid workers in a deadly reign of terror, torture and beheadings, and who has become infamous to T.V. viewers around the world, as Jihadi Mick?

Professor Sir Richard Prendergast, the famous home office expert on facial reconstruction tells the Sun in an exclusive interview that he believes "in all probability it is".

Below is our artist's impression of what he might look like today and details of the huge reward we are offering for information leading to his arrest.

***

Getting out of LAX took an hour longer than expected as someone had accidentally set off a security alarm all over the airport by carelessly backing a small bus into an alarmed guard post at the fire department's emergency runway access gate. Alistair was relieved that his 'becoming famous' face did not start up another alert and cost him more hours of wasted time. Yes, he'd had some sleep on the plane, but the thought of a warm, soft, hotel bed with a pre-booked choice of firmness of the mattress and pillows, really sounded good, especially after a few G and Ts too many during the long flight. His P.A. had thoughtfully organised a car and driver to take him north to the hotel. Everything he needed for the whole trip, including a large quantity of 'Play' dollars, was carefully split between his $895, Montblanc, Meisterstuck, black leather briefcase, that he carried everywhere, and his battered metallic blue Samsonite four- wheeler that took the brunt of any hold damage, stickers and airport handling.

Lying in the darkness of his comfortable suite Alistair kept thinking about the T.V. show he had seen on the aircraft. There was something about that old Irish woman and her story that made him feel deeply uncomfortable. In fact, despite the air-conditioning running quietly in the background, his forehead had begun to sweat and he had become aware of his own heartbeat. Never mind, he thought, it was probably only the revenge of the gin and tonics, and anyway, he was in his own show tomorrow in front of paying customers in a big dealership. He would need to be sharp, fresh and presentable. Who knows, he thought, there might even be a replacement for George amongst the staff in the dealerships he was going to visit. No more crazy journeys from New York. That was a nice idea to go back to sleep on.

CHAPTER 11

The big room in the Union Hotel was set out in conference style, with a spare chair occupying every spare space. People had started to arrive early. Stopping to talk to neighbours they hadn't seen for a while before filing through the snubbed open, tall double doors into the well-lit room and settling into the red-cushioned, 'wedding guest', narrow chairs that formed the middle and back rows. In front of the audience was a long catering type table covered in a clean white tablecloth. Behind the table was an old style school blackboard screwed onto a sturdy, galvanised steel stand resting on castors. There was also an American flag attached to an arrow-straight, mahogany pole, draped with a faded gold rope and topped with two fringed tassels. The two, ornate, high-backed, dark wooden chairs, set up for the speakers to use, along with the flag, were the only items rescued from a fire in the old mayor's office some fifty years earlier and were always used by the hotel for ceremonies and big occasions.

A banner announcing 'Molinos Ridge welcomes you'. a leftover from the annual bike event, was hung, with plastic cable ties, over the entrance to the hotel. Quite what the welcome was going to be for the visiting spokesperson from the oil company, was yet to be seen, thought Sheriff Culzean.

A few of the big landowners boldly sat in the front rows, both to show their place in local society and because they were older than the majority of the population and could neither see nor hear very clearly. The Sheriff immediately noticed a couple of those in the front row had ignored the hotel's request to leave their guns behind for this meeting and he spoke softly to them.

"We were hoping that you, Sir, and you, Sir, could set an example for us, on the gun front. Yes, I know what the law says about it. But if we allow you guys to be showing a gun, everyone can, and that includes some known troublemakers if you know who I mean. Yes Sir, I very much appreciate that kind gesture. I'll keep them safe and return them to you when we're finished."

After a long wait, the crowd began to become impatient. Carlton and the hotel's nervous Assistant Manager stood in front of the covered table and Carlton spoke, "As you can see, the representative of Anglo American does not appear to be here yet. I have asked my deputy to head down the southern turnpike to see if she can spot him in case his car has broken down or something like that. So I would ask you all to be patient until she reports back. Pastor, perhaps you could lead us in a song or two to pass the time."

As the Pastor rose to his feet and turned to face the crowd, an elderly woman's voice shouted huskily from the back, "Is he driving a new Cadillac?"

As the whole crowd turned to look at her,

Carlton asked, "Why, have you seen him?"

"As I was leaving my home tonight, I noticed that someone had badly parked a brand new black Cadillac near to the entrance of my drive. I would have stopped and looked, but I was on my way here and wanted to get a good seat."

The palm shaped combined microphone and speaker on a curled wire, clipped to Carlton's uniform, pinged twice and began to hiss. "Yeah Rose, have you found him?"

"Would the lady who spoke earlier please stay behind and if our doctor is in the audience, Sir, I am going to need your help. The rest of you, I'm sorry but our meeting is cancelled, so please will you all go home and we will keep you informed. There is nothing for you to be concerned about, please go home."

Carlton switched on the roof top light bar and all the pursuit lights on his Chevrolet Suburban black and white Sheriff's car then lurched out the car park heading fast out of town, with the invited doctor and the uninvited local journalist close behind, both doing their best to keep up in their own less powerful four wheel drives.

As he approached Rose's Crown Victoria, black and white, he could see that the black Cadillac was stuck nose first into an overgrown thorny bush and this was causing some damage to the glossy black paint on the front of the car. Walking closer, he spotted the Hertz, 'no.1 club', yellow and black sticker on a corner of the back window and a yellow 'H14', Hertz swing ticket hanging from the rear view mirror inside the big sedan. All this indicated to Carlton that it was a hired car which had been collected by someone in a hurry. It was probably the missing oilman right enough.

Rose pulled on her thick, black leather gloves and held the thorn bush back and away from the big front grill. This revealed a sizeable bullet hole straight through the chrome bars of the grill. Rose could see that the bullet had passed through the top of the radiator and was resting on the front of the plastic engine cover which capped off the engine. The movement had caused some blue-green coolant to trickle very slightly out of a cracked hose which then dropped and disappeared into the bone dry ground below. In the driver's seat, slumped across the exploded airbag steering wheel lay the driver. He was a balding white man of around sixty years old, whose smashed yellow metal and tortoise shell glasses were thrown across the dashboard. There was a large part of the back of his head missing. His I-pad and I-phone had jumped off the passenger seat and were wedged together against the passenger door. There was a lot of brain matter all over the car, but very little blood except on the headlining.

"Are you alright Rose? I know it's not the nicest thing to find out on the road at night but the Doc and I are here now so you don't have to look any more. Maybe you could keep our journalist friend behind a line, while I take a few pictures and try to find out, for sure, who this is. Oh, and Rose, if it's who I think it is, you'd better call the hotel and tell the old woman who lives here to stay in town tonight. This place will be overrun with all sorts of people from all over the County by the morning."

"I can do that, but remember I'm the one who's trained in this," said Rose, who had spent two years in the L.A. P.D. before returning to work with her 'family firm', as she called it, in Molinos Ridge.

***

One of the things Alistair actually liked about being back on the road was a hotel breakfast. He had slept really well and had given himself enough time to properly indulge. Several strong cups of English Breakfast tea, bacon, hash browns, sausage, mushrooms, toast and butter followed by some pancakes with maple syrup was, in his opinion, the perfect result of the 'special relationship' between his birth country of Great Britain and his adopted homeland of the U.S.A.

Jools ran the house in New Jersey really well, but with a full time career and two boys to get to school, breakfast often consisted of a long, strong coffee and a diet biscuit before putting on a seatbelt and heading out. Alistair had often mentioned the idea of getting in some help, but despite the fact that the house was big enough and they could afford it, Jools didn't want strangers in her home and, as far as the discussion was concerned, that was the end of it. When it came to the house, in Alistair's opinion, Jool's word was law.

After breakfast, Alistair returned to his suite in order to 'dress to impress'. It was always important to be well groomed, but especially so when visiting a dealership for the first time in one of America's richest cities.

A white Gucci shirt with a dark grey, narrow, Burberry London tie started the ensemble. He topped this with a three-piece, grey, box check, Dolce and Gabbana formal suit. The finishing touches were provided by a red and white polka dot, Drakes pocket square with less than an inch showing above his top pocket. Then lastly a bit of tie jewellery in the shape of a Brown Brothers clip which Jools had brought back for him, following a lunch time trip with a new client to the Neiman Marcus store in Elizabeth, a couple of weeks earlier.

A quick look in the full length mirror confirmed the suitability of his choices although he considered that the current fashion for very narrow trousers worked a lot better on shorter people.

***

As both Alistair and Jools McKenzie owed their success, in no small part, to having a great start in life, based around an excellent tertiary education, the importance they placed on the education of their sons was considered by them to be paramount to their family values. Each of the boys had a fully equipped bedroom to themselves with all the latest technology that money could buy and big screens to watch on.

They each had a regular routine of after school study with the oldest son, Alistair junior or 'Al' as he preferred to be called, the more enthusiastic of the two siblings. Aware of the dangers that the internet could pose, Jools liked to drop in now and then, to see what they were working on and lend a hand if required.

"Do you want anything to eat or drink, brought up to your room, Al?" asked Jools, using the inbuilt videocom system in the large house.

"No mom, I'm fine," was the reply.

"Do you mind if I join you, I've put out some of your father's favourite toffee popcorn into a bowl for you?"

"Sure Mom, I'd like some."

Jools put the popcorn into a plastic serving bowl and, taking the tops off two classic diet Coke bottles, and placing everything on a silver tray, she set out for Al's room in the east wing of the spacious house.

After consuming a couple of big handfuls of popcorn and most of her Coke, Jools took an interest in a photo of a Jihadist wearing a black scarf over the bottom of his face that Al had showing on his screen.

"You're not thinking of joining them are you? Because I can assure you there wouldn't be any popcorn or Coke in that camp, only rice and water." Two things Al didn't like very much.

"No Mom, just a bit of research for my school project. That's Jihadi Mick. The one who looks like Dad!"

"The project is called Evil men in history. Most of the other guys have gone for Hitler and Genghis Khan and other dudes like that from way back. I thought it would be cool to do someone who is on T.V. right now."

"So what have you found so far?"

"Well they say that he's really this dude from Belfast in Northern Ireland. And this bit's really cool. This guy is his brother and he looks just like me!" Al said, pointing to the screen. "Also he was born in September 1975 exactly the same as dad."

Jools stared at the family photos from Belfast and thought about the similarities in looks to her husband and sons, and the coincidences of the birth month and year.

"Mom, I could really do with something else in the way of information. Would it be alright if I contacted that family to find out more about what sent him bananas in the first place?"

"Al, I don't think it's a good idea for a thirteen year old to be contacting the family of a terrorist, even if it is for a school project. This whole thing interests me though. There are so many coincidences, and the way they all look!"

"Mom, would you do it for me. It doesn't have to be in for another week and Mr. Bronstein is always telling us not to rely only on the internet for our research."

"Alright, I'll see what I can find out for you. But I can't promise anything, so keep working on it, even without my help."

Jools headed back to her kitchen to see what other 'bribes' she could use to check on her younger son. As she walked down the grand curved staircase, holding on to the detailed metal balustrade with its elm wood capping, she stopped for a moment to take in a strong sense of déjà vu before returning to her huge 'to-do' list.

***

In the hallway of a small, red-brick, terraced house in Belfast a personalised embossed envelope sporting an airmail stamp and containing a letter, awaited its occupants. It sat on the coir mat behind the front door along with adverts for a hearing aid service, a new curry delivery restaurant, double glazed replacement doors and an overdue, red printed telephone bill from B.T.

It was a letter that would change a number of people's lives. The last paragraph read:-

And I hope you don't mind me writing to you out of the blue like this, but because your son Daniel bears <u>such</u> a striking resemblance to my husband, I wanted to telephone you to see if he is, in any way related to your family. A client of mine works for the television company you spoke to and, in complete confidence, he gave me your number. If possible, I would like to phone you on Wednesday around six in the evening, your time. I hope that will suit you.

I look forward to talking to you.

Best Regards from New Jersey, U.S.A.

Jools Mackenzie.

Mrs Julia Mackenzie.

CHAPTER 12

The journey from Syria to Turkey was even easier than he had first expected. Having discarded his 'Press' waistcoat in a roadside bin he was dressed only in black trousers and a black, long sleeved T-shirt. Yousef decided he needed a few more items of clothing to deal with the cold wind that blew through southern Turkey. He also wanted to fit in a little better with the locals, almost all of whom were at least six inches shorter that him.

Zeynep's shop was stuffed full of the most eclectic collection of items from through the ages that Yousef had ever seen. Old television sets sat on top of neat string-bound piles of National Geographic magazines in various languages. Ladies hats mingled with clear and coloured glass vases. Wardrobes in a multitude of shapes and sizes sat on the stone floor in front of an assortment of mirrors. An early Nintendo set, some Star Wars figures bereft of paint and a large, badly executed painting of a local fishing boat rested on a damaged, grey metal, office desk, all of which were for sale. The strong smell of black Turkish tobacco, even blacker sweet local coffee and second-hand mustiness pervaded the atmosphere of the shop and everything in it.

Near to the open corner entrance was a long, well stuffed rail of pre-owned men's clothing. I won't find trousers to fit me here but a jacket and a scarf are just what I need, thought Yousef as he systematically went through the rail to search for something suitable.

After trying on a few items, he settled on a grey padded anorak which had once belonged to an employee of the Turkish Petroleum company and had the distinctive 'T.P.', red and white logo on the sleeves. A light blue, informal cotton shirt with a button-down soft collar and a plain, maroon coloured scarf completed the look of a local workman, possibly from a petrol station or the port. After Yousef agreed to leave his black T-shirt, as a trade in, Zeynep accepted a price of 37 Lira equating to about $15 U.S.

Winding his way down the narrow streets towards the little harbour, Yousef pulled the A4 list that Mohammed had prepared for him out from his backpack.

SPREE IV.

Registered in Kiel.   27mtr; Twin screw motor/sailor diesel yacht. Contact: Matias Schmidt: $5,000 U.S. in cash.

As Yousef walked around the harbour there was no sign of the Spree IV. He carefully examined every boat for the name or the type of vessel in case the name had been changed, but without luck. Near the entrance to the stone pier, a recently whitewashed two storey building had a sign on it showing an official crest and saying in big blue letters 'Liman Reisi', in Turkish, then in small black letters underneath in English, Harbour Master.

Yousef thought long and hard before climbing the metal stair that ran up the side of the building to the open door leading to the office. In his back pack was a lot of cash and a well-worn Colt .38, special pistol. He decided to talk first and use a bit of cash if needed. If all else failed, the Colt would do just what the old adverts claimed and be the equaliser, providing him the opportunity of a fast exit from the office and even faster lurch down the metal exterior stairs to freedom.

As he entered the small office through the open door he immediately noticed the poster on the wall showing the green star and crescent symbol popular with older Turkish Muslims. Beside it, a torn poster, carefully repaired with sticky tape, bore the word 'Allah', expressed in modern calligraphic script. And lastly, an up-to-date, large, glossy calendar with a photo of Mecca was held aloft by a metal pin on the wall behind the small wooden desk.

Seated behind the desk in a well-worn black leather chair was a very thin bespectacled man wearing a shabby, uniform shirt. In front of him lay a set of long, Russian made binoculars beside their scratched, brown leather case.

"Salam," said Yousef.

"You are English?" enquired the official.

"Irish actually," replied Yousef.

"Can I help you?" enquired the official, in perfect English.

"I'm looking for a boat. The Spree IV out of Kiel."

"Why do you want this particular boat?" asked the official.

The boat being missing and the caginess of the official tipped off Yousef to be especially cautious in his reply.

"I'm a journalist on a story. Has something happened?"

"You don't look like a journalist?"

"Yes," replied Yousef. "I find that helps."

"You're too late," said the official. "All the action was two days ago. The drugs squad were here and took away the German crew and confiscated the boat."

"Dammit," said Yousef. "That's my story blown and I paid a lot for the tip as well!"

The mention of a lot of money caused the officials eyes to open wide behind his glasses.

"I don't suppose you have a story for me?" Yousef asked, opening then folding two crisp new 100 Lira notes into the red velvet interior of the open binocular case on the desk.

"What kind of story would you like?" asked the official as he swiftly closed the case while looking Yousef straight in the eyes. He then silently placed the case under his desk.

"People smuggling. I would like to do a story on

people who can get you from this harbour over to Cyprus for cash. I would pay a lot to write a story like that. You know, take part in the journey and write my memoirs about the trip afterwards."

"There is a ferry leaves here every other day?" quizzed the official.

"Yes," replied Yousef. "But what if your landing on Cyprus was to be without the attention of the authorities?"

"But you are Irish, you can travel to Cyprus any time you like?"

"Exactly, so there is no real risk for anyone. Just a good bit of research for my editor and some Lira for a local boat owner."

"My brother has a boat. How much would you pay and when do you want to go?" asked the official with an obvious sound of excitement in his voice.

"Shall we say $1,000 U.S. dollars and can we sail at high tide tonight?"

"If you have this amount of cash, I can make the arrangement for you."

"Half when I get on the boat and half when I safely land on Greek Cyprus without being spotted by anyone."

"Akkus, my brother is playing chess outside the coffee shop across the street. You can see him from here. He is the one who is as fat as I am thin. Come with me now and I will introduce you."

As Akkus showed Yousef round the boat and down the broad stairs to his cabin, he was surprised at how luxurious the interior of the two masted, 28 metre long, traditional Turkish gulet was. Yousef stopped in front of the full-length, bevelled glass mirror on his cabin's main wardrobe and thought, I need a shave. I should have bought some razors back in Silifke. Perhaps our Captain has a new one? Then again, I will be travelling to California. Maybe a bit of designer stubble will look good on me out there.

As he settled in for the journey he thought he would have a look at Mohammad's email account on Hotmail. Mohammad may be spread across the desert in small pieces by now, but there could be some messages for him that would be useful. While they were still tied up in the harbour, there was a chance he could get some sort of signal.

Yousef went down the list in date order. An advert for a 20% discount at Melia Hotels group, a hair re-growth treatment clinic. He won't need that now, thought Yousef. There was also an email from the helpful cousin in America.

"Hi Mo. Hope your friend liked the chocolates and the card I sent. Did it all arrive safely? Achmed."

Yousef replied. "Yes cousin Achmed. It was very good of you. My friend Y will not need the card now, but enjoyed the sweets. He wants you to meet him when he arrives in America. Go to a town called… Yousef stopped writing for a moment and picked at random on Google maps, a small 'hick' town east of Millers Mountain, Molinos Ridge. Make sure his gun collection is in good condition and ready for inspection.

All of this is of the most importance to us both. If you love your family, you will do this. Y will cover all your costs and more when he gets there. Thanks for your help. Mo."

Yousef just managed to send a follow on email to Achmed giving a detailed description of 'Y' including his soft Northern Irish accent, before the signal was lost as the 450 horse power Volvo Penta main engine thrummed up to full revs and pushed the gulet out of the harbour and on to its steady cruising speed of twelve knots. The distance from Tasucu port, near Silifke, to the coast of Cyprus was around a hundred and thirty miles, so Yousef decided to rest and wake in around four hours.

***

The Woodlands Hills dealership had certainly pulled out all the stops for both the launch and Alistair's visit. Every used car had their doors wide open across the huge lot. The grounds wrapped around the front of the showroom had flags waving from poles secured under the front wheels. The local high school marching band was keeping the crowd happy by playing a medley of traditional American military music by John Phillip Sousa including 'stars and stripes forever'. As Alistair's chauffeured Lincoln sedan pulled up in front of the showroom entrance, a signal went up from the bandmaster and the music immediately changed to a slightly jazzy version of 'Scotland the brave'.

Alistair had, for some reason, and quite unusually for him, been feeling a little sensitive for the previous few hours and the sound of this tribute to him almost brought a tear to his eye. The General Manager had all the sales and office staff lined up in a row as if they would be meeting Prince Charles at a Royal variety performance in London. Alistair soon recovered his composure and began to buy into the moment. He joined the owners' party on the reinforced, temporary stage that housed one of the new coupe's, under a huge flag, all of which looked to Alistair more like a funeral for a fallen war hero at Arlington National Cemetery, rather than a car unveiling. After a few introductions, he was invited to pull the cord which operated an overhead winch, lifting the flag to reveal the new car in all of its dark blue over gold, metallic splendour. With over two hundred and fifty former customers, local car enthusiasts and staff, many who had only turned up on the back of a promise of valuable prizes and a free lunch, it took a few moments for the applause and general noise to die down.

Alistair addressed the crowd, "Firstly, I would like to thank Mr. Cohen, his family and his staff for inviting me today and for the wonderful welcome you have all given to me. Especially the members of your fabulous high school band for the really brilliant tribute they made just now both to me and to my place of birth, which some of you will know, was Scotland."

Alistair went on to talk about the new car, the 'one-off' re-launch for the historic brand, and the rest of the models available in the broader range from Ford, before handing back to his hosts to announce the activities and prizes on offer.

Mr. Cohen asked, "Would people holding a red invite, queue first, for the buffet, which Mrs Edelman's kosher catering company is now serving."

And, as he said it, the large crowd armed with red invites surged forward grabbing plates and eagerly started to go through the spread of food like a hoard of educated locusts.

The activities seemed to last forever. Guess the weight of this or how many beans in that, until the big crowd eventually started to run out of luck or interest and went home. By the closing stages, Alistair had eaten enough blinis to last him a lifetime and he now really wanted a big steak and a bigger glass of good Californian red wine to wash it down. He had spotted something or rather someone he liked. One of the salespeople at the dealership, Rupert, was very organised and great with customers. Also, he had the most gorgeous, tall, slim, African American, young wife with him, supporting her husband at the event. A possible replacement for George? Alistair thought again, about the young wife, then remembering his motto, 'don't mix business with pleasure', he decided it was best to leave it. That steak and a wine or three was a definite though, he thought, as he sat, once again, in splendour in the back of the firms, top of the range, demonstrator Lincoln sedan, listening to its smooth V8 growl while it made stately progress back to his nearby hotel.

***

Brenda McConnell poured herself a small glass of Bushmills and waited for the last family member to leave through the front door of her terraced house before sitting at her wooden kitchen table. She started to write down the questions that had been haunting her since the surprise letter from America arrived on her doorstep.

Where should I start? she wondered. Everything Brenda was about to write brought back memories she had suppressed for almost all of her adult life. She was embarrassed, ashamed and vulnerable in a way that she had not been in decades.

This woman wants answers. That's what we all want, she thought, as she carefully tore the blank part off of a large white envelope and, with tears brimming up in her eyes, headed it up, 'Darren.'

Her first question would seem to Jools an unusual one, but for Brenda, was entirely the logical place to start.

Is your husband a Roman Catholic or was he brought up as one?

When is his birthday, what date?

Is he healthy and has he had a happy life?

And lastly.

Do you have any children of your own or do you plan to have any?

Brenda already thought she knew the answers, but was deeply worried about the impact that both families would have to face if the answers Jools gave caused the secret truth, suppressed all those years, to be revealed. As the time passed ever more slowly until six o'clock, Belfast time, Brenda became more and more tense. She could taste the alcohol and tears on her lips. The temptation to finish her bottle of Bushmills was great, but Brenda wanted to make a good first impression and soon went back to strong cups of Typhoo tea and buttered McVities digestive biscuits to bolster up her spirits and await the long distance call.

CHAPTER 13

Despite the comfort offered by the best bed he had lain on for many months, Yousef found it hard to sleep. The movement of the boat and the creaking of the wooden hull, along with the gentle background thrum and burr of the engine all contrived to keep him awake. In all his time training and fighting as a Jihadi, he had developed heightened senses to movement near him and a natural mistrust of other people around him. His host had prepared for him a glass of beer and insisted that he drink up. Yousef, not to appear to be impolite, said he would drink it later, however, as a strict Muslim disposed of it down the toilet, before returning the empty glass to his bedside cabinet.

Yousef had some questions as well. Why was the captain so keen to take him on such a risky journey? Also, he felt that the deck hand, the only other crew member on board, spent a second or two too many checking out Yousef's back pack with his cash and new lap top in it, when he partially opened it to hand over the $500 half payment at the start of the trip.

He pulled back the red duvet on the bed, took the revolver from his pack and pushed it into his belt. Then he put the pack into the bed and piled the pillows up to look as if he was still sleeping there.

He clambered into the wardrobe and used one of

the metal coat hangers to hold the door open a couple of inches, just enough to see without being seen.

His hunch was right. Very quietly the captain and the deck hand entered the room. The captain held a heavy, old, English revolver and the deck hand had a cosh and a set of handcuffs. As they crept forward towards, what they thought, was a sleeping victim. Yousef kicked open the wardrobe door and put two bullets into the captain's head and the remaining four into the chest of his accomplice.

The fat captain slumped onto the bed while the other man wriggled in pain, screaming and bleeding all over the cabin floor. Yousef walked slowly over to the Captain and helped himself to his gun. He then took out the knife from his backpack and slit the other man's throat with his customary single arm movement.

In the wheelhouse all the lights and the rev counter proved that the engine was still running perfectly and the crewman had secured the big aluminium wheel by a cord to maintain the chosen course.

Yousef had no idea how to control such a big vessel, so he pushed forward the throttle lever to the point where the engine was just turning over and, leaving the wheel tethered, he decided to explore and see what he could find. At the stern was a clinker-built, wooden service dingy held in place by powered davits with a very new looking Suzuki, four horsepower, four stroke outboard motor and an auxiliary eighty-five litre fuel tank.

In the Captain's cabin Yousef found his $500 and around another 10,000 more in a mixture of lira and Euros. He also found a ball gag, several shapes of rubber dildo, a dozen male bondage magazines, an HP photo printer and a series of photos that looked like they were taken on board, each of a different young man in handcuffs, stripped to his underwear, tethered and being beaten, whipped and forced to have oral and anal sex with a number of older men, presumably paying guests. One of the photos also showed an attractive, slim, dark haired girl going through the same ordeal. Presumably the captain had managed to capture and drug a young couple on board. Yousef decided to keep the photos of the girl as they were much more to his taste.

He realised how lucky he had been that he was unable to sleep on board and his beliefs had stopped him from taking the drink. Once again he prayed and thanked Allah for his deliverance and took it as a holy sign of the importance of his mission to Groom Lake and area 51.

The question he now asked himself was, 'where are we?' as he pulled the chrome throttle lever towards him drawing higher revs from the engine and turned the wheel until the dashboard electronic compass read due south.

***

Jed Nordstrom loved his new Beechcraft Bonanza G36. With its 18,500 ft. ceiling and 200mph performance it was the ideal, comfortable and economical, single engine aircraft to operate in the dangerous mountainous conditions that surrounded the single tarmac airstrip and hanger, that he proudly called Nordstrom Airport. As Jed put it, he bought the plane, brand new from the factory, chose the four leather seat and extra luggage capacity configuration, and paid extra to upgrade the standard Garmin avionics up to full military standard, as he called it, to cope with the extreme changes in conditions. He had personally experienced these conditions on numerous occasions, boring the locals in the town bar half to sleep, retelling stories of his exploits in conquering the infamous Nevada triangle.

When asked, 'Did you ever see any sign of Steve Fossett?' (The billionaire aviator whose plane went missing from the area in 2007), Jed always replied, 'Well sure I do. I give him a tip of my wings and a wave, every time I've gone past his ranch at Yerington.'

Jed carefully studied the latest one, three and seven day weather forecast from the National Weather service and planned to use the most direct route to C.S.N. Carson City Airport. C.S.N. was one of three airports that could serve the city, but was the most user-friendly for a small operator like him. They also had a good, fast refuelling operation which would be really convenient when doing both legs of a flight on the same day. This was made possible because the P.A. of the New York City slicker, as he called Alistair, had booked and paid for the whole trip in full, in advance.

Jed called around the local business contacts on his phone: "Yep, planes going to be empty apart from one guy and his suitcase. Well, if you need anything dropped off or picked up in Carson on that day, I have the space and most of the costs are already covered, so I can give you a real good neighbour price.

"Yeah, I can do a payload of that weight, so long as we can fit it in the aircraft. All individual packs. Sure, any time after 14.00 and before 19.00 at C.S.N. to give me time to do all the checks. No… thank you."

**

Sheriff Culzean waited until his sister was well down the lane ushering the reporter to a spot where he could not interfere, before putting on a pair of the doctor's surgical gloves and reaching in to the car to search the dead man's trousers for his wallet.

"Doc, could you go back and ask Rose to call the state police and tell them what's going on here?"

As soon as the Doctor was also out of sight he checked out the notes compartment of the dead man's wallet. Carlton quickly and silently counted out three hundred and sixty-five dollars. He separated two hundred dollars and put them swiftly into his own wallet before returning the rest and examining the card sections. The many credit cards, memberships, and Anglo American business cards, all in the same name, told him that this was the oilman alright and robbery was not the motive. Carlton thought about how shocked he was when his late father imposed what he called, a bit of local taxation, in front of him for the first time and told him that the real crime was how badly paid a small town Sheriff was. Oh, and getting caught of course, that would be criminal.

Carlton then added to his nightly tally by pocketing a crisp new $100 dollar bill, round the back of his Suburban, black and white, for the widows and orphans, as he put it. Accepting this from the previously banished journalist, for confirming the identity of the dead man and stating that he died from a single gunshot through his open driver's door window. Probably from an assailant sitting or crouching on the embankment with what was, more than likely, a rifle and at quite close range.

Carlton returned to the black Cadillac to take more photographs using his Nokia windows phone. Then he opened the car's trunk electronically using the dash switch, for a quick look, before closing it all up again to wait for a full forensic S.O.C. squad and an ambulance to arrive up from the city.

***

Achmed managed to convince his boss to give him a week's holiday and put in for the same time for his sister, Noor, to go with him. His boss had never made any suggestions or even looked at Noor the wrong way, but Achmed felt it was safer for her to come with. They both knew the type of things their cousin Mohammed was involved with in Syria and both of them had grown up with guns and had occasion to use them before they came to the relative safety of a millionaire's estate in Los Angeles. The boss had told them they could use any of the vehicles in his garage, except the Packard, the Duesenberg or his 1937 knucklehead Harley Davidson bike. Achmed decided to borrow the new, white, Chevrolet Malibu sedan. Firstly, because it was the car he used most often to go to the local market for groceries, but also because it would draw the least attention out on the road. After a quick look on the internet, Noor was able to secure two, twin rooms for single occupancy at the Union hotel, on a bed and breakfast basis. Another look on the web found them a pawnbroker along the route who kept an extensive array of sporting weapons and pre-owned handguns, always in stock. Achmed made a careful note of Mohammed's description of Yousef, put together all the documentation needed for him and his sister to buy guns, and cashed out almost all their savings before embarking northwards on their journey.

"This place we are heading for looks nice," commented Achmed, half an hour into the journey.

"I hope we can eat halal there," replied Noor.

"I'm sure we can find something to eat there, but just in case, when we stop to buy guns, we can shop for our food at the same time," reassured Achmed. "You know what we may be asked to do, you do know?" asked Achmed.

"I am not ready to be a martyr, yet, but I will kill if we need to," replied Noor.

Nothing more was said on the subject and after an hour on the road they arrived at the turnoff and the short driveway into Tri-Western Pawn and Loan's long, narrow and very secure premises. The website didn't lie and the variety of guns for sale was really huge. Achmed bought one for himself and one for Yousef, a pair of .40 Glock G23 Gen 2 semi auto pistols with night sights. Noor chose a .40 Walther PPQ M2 which suited her smaller hands.

They both thought that one of the best balanced rifles in the store was a Browning A bolt II stalker 7mm rem mag with a 26inch barrel and the Boss system.

The shop keeper pointed out, "They only made this model with this barrel for a short time and this one's in its original box. It's sure to become a collector's item and if you go for all four items, I can do an excellent deal for you on ammo and I can throw in this deluxe, Jack Pyke game bag, as part of the deal."

Achmed got him to throw in a wooden-handled hunting knife to make the deal even sweeter before shaking hands and handing over his credit card for $2,332.00 along with his driving license with its impressive Holmby Hills mansion address.

The game bag came in useful at the next grocery store where the siblings stocked up on several small bottles of diet Seven Up, fresh orange juice, organic milk, chick peas to make humus, avocados and two loaves of organic rye bread. By the time they reached the hotel, three police cars, two T.V. trucks, an ambulance from the state Coroners department and the doctors 4x4 had arrived in a hurry and all were hastily abandoned near to the hotel entrance with their occupants holding impromptu meetings in and around the hotel's well-stocked bar.

"Should we stop?" asked Noor, nervously.

"I don't think any of this is for us and it's too early for Yousef. Leave the guns in the car and stick to our story," said Achmed in his most reassuring voice.

At the reception Achmed booked them in and

casually asked, "What's all the fuss about?"

The Deputy Manager replied, "Oh, nothing for you to worry about, Sir, just a local difficulty about a guest speaker who crashed his car on his way here. Would you like me to show you to your rooms? They're next to each other on the second floor, 216 and 217. I see you have a hunting bag. I have one like that. Are you here to hunt?"

"No," replied Achmed. "My sister and I are on a special diet and it's an ideal way for us to carry food. "Neither of us likes guns," he added for good measure as he surveyed the view from his window with a marksman's eye.

CHAPTER 14

As the sun started to come up and glint off the highly varnished wood surfaces of the gulet, Yousef could see the outline of land appearing in the distance. Was it Turkey, Cyprus or, Allah forbid, Syria once again? He was starting to get hungry and had not found any food on board that he could eat. A quick look around the galley had revealed a large, key opened, tin of 'Ye Olde Oak' brand of ham, which must have belonged to a previous passenger. The sight of this object made him feel disgusted and prevented him from a further search of the galley cupboards. He was also anxious not to be found on board by any authorities. With two dead bodies, loads of cash, two pistols, one of which was previously fired and all the sexual material downstairs, even he couldn't come up with a convincing story that matched what they would find if they boarded the boat.

***

Brenda McConnell had told all the members of her family to make themselves scarce at six o'clock that night as she was expecting an important phone call from the personnel at Asda about a full-time cleaning job and she didn't want their entire racket going on in the background.

In her luxury home in Upper Saddle River, New Jersey, Jools McKenzie was having her third small cup of Rombouts original roast, strong filter coffee, to help her stay awake for her half past midnight call to Ireland. Fuelled more by curiosity than anything else, Jools didn't know what to expect or even if anyone would answer the phone. After all, there was no way of knowing if her letter had even been received, let alone taken with any degree of seriousness.

Meanwhile Alistair was on his tablet, reading emails from Bernice sent from the New York office.

'The only other thing I need to tell you is that Big Jim from Carson City has been on his cell phone to ask if he can treat you to a special dinner after their launch. He seemed very excited about it. Something called the meal of your life, at the famous Little Amsterdam Restaurant. I told him it was O.K. provided he got you back to the C.S.N. airport not a minute later than 19.00 as that's when I have arranged for you and Mr. Nordstrom to fly back. I accepted it on your behalf and you will find it confirmed in your Penzu Diary.'

'Thanks, Bernice,' answered Alistair, with his usual degree of brevity when responding to her highly detailed emails.

Having dealt with business, Alistair's thoughts moved on to more recreational pursuits. The tablet he was using was his own property, so he was able to use it to visit websites that would have resulted in a disciplinary hearing at work, if he was discovered using the company's machine for such purpose.

How embarrassing would that be, thought Alistair, as he settled onto the king size hotel bed to see what was on offer near to the hotel. A quick look through using a Google search of 'Los Angeles contacts' and words like 'Brothel' brought more warnings than answers. There were, however, a lot of 'adult' clubs on offer. Some exclusively gay, which didn't interest him, and one that was very long established, called the Spearmint Rhino, Gentleman's Club. The website had over twenty pictures for him to look at. Only in Los Angeles could you pay to watch a variety of really cracking looking girls dancing for you, half naked, and at the end up, when you are at your most horny, you settle up your bill and go home, thought Alistair. The message on the website invited him to 'ask any L.A. taxi driver to bring you here,' and it did offer Alistair some level of temptation. But then he thought about his favourite Paradise club in Stuttgart, Germany. There he received at the front desk a year's membership for only fifty euros, a free grand buffet meal, a selection of movies and his choice of over twenty five willing girls from all over Europe, who, for another forty euros each, would do almost anything on a man's list. And in Germany, at least, the whole thing is completely legal so he wasn't risking spending the night in a drug riddled L.A. jail, or worse still, getting shot by a gang member in a hoodie, just for being on the wrong neighbourhood street. Back in New York he could get exactly what he asked for with very little risk and no commitment so long as he continued to be able to afford to pay New York prices.

Alistair thought long and hard about it, but decided to stay put and do some more work. After all, in a few days he would be back in New Jersey with Jools and, at any time he wanted, back in New York in a private apartment having fun with Felice.

***

Yousef realised that his next move was going to involve an element of chance. Allah had guided and saved him more than once in the last few days. He washed and using the boat's compass to face Mecca, knelt down and prayed. He really started to believe that his mission was making him invincible and the risk he was about to take was not really much of a risk at all.

Yousef pointed the boat due north and cut the engine. Tying the aluminium wheel to the throttle lever tightly with a cord, he gathered his things and walked to the back of the gulet then gradually lowered the service boat into the calm water. After clambering into the small boat, he cut it free and started the engine with its push button electric start, then pulled away from the gulet in exactly the opposite direction to where the yacht was now pointing and headed to where, a few moments earlier, he had made sight of the outline of land.

He took off the grey, padded jacket and threw it into the water then tied the red scarf round his neck in the 'continental' style he had seen stylish people wearing on T.V. As he got closer to shore he realised that he was sailing towards a busy holiday resort. Before long, he started to pull back on the throttle so as to make less of an entrance and to avoid crashing into some of the braver swimmers who had ventured further from the shore. Ahead of him was a narrow wooden jetty and Yousef docked near to the end of it. He tied up the boat and jumped onto the first of two attached wooden steps. As he walked along the jetty he heard English being spoken and stopped to speak to a teenage boy who was sitting, dangling his legs over the side.

"Are you English?" he asked the boy.

"Yeah, what of it?" the boy replied in a broad Liverpool accent.

"What town is this?" Yousef enquired.

"Protaras," the boy replied.

"In Cyprus?" asked Yousef

"No, on Mars," answered the boy confidently, putting his finger to his head and indicating that Yousef was a bit mad. Yousef was not used to being spoken to that way. He stopped and looked hard at the boy for a moment and thought about how easy it would be to quietly slit his worthless throat and tip him gently forward into the water. He could be well down the wooden pier before anyone had even noticed the splash. Even though he felt certain that he would be doing his parents, his school and the world a favour by ridding them of this pest, he realised it would be the wrong thing for him to do at this time, especially when he needed to blend in with the tourists on the island. If he saw him on his own at a different time, then it would be a different matter, he thought.

He remembered Mohammed's words about it being almost more important where you're coming from than where you are going to from the point of view of fooling the border guards. With this in mind he resolved to become a typical tourist, in appearance, at least.

In amongst the usual roadside tourist shops that spilled out onto the street selling inflatable toys, sun glasses and tanning cream was a long established shop selling shoes, leather belts and bags. Yousef bought from the old Hindu owner a large, lightweight, blue-coloured, four wheeled suitcase and putting his backpack inside it he then wheeled it through the glass and white marble open entrance of the Lacoste concession store next door where, with the help of an attractive young female assistant, he transformed himself into a well-off British tourist, just arrived, to start his annual week's holiday. His next move was to jump into a local taxi and, after asking the driver which hotels dealt with Thomson Holidays, travelled in the cab the impossibly short journey to the Anais Bay, three star hotel, where he kept the cab's meter running while he enquired if they had a room for him for the next three nights. After carefully checking that the passport and the credit card he was about to hand over to the receptionist had matching names, he booked in. Then he paid the cab, left the case in the comfortable twin bedded room and, with his cash and guns carefully stuffed into the small, room safe behind the sliding, mirrored door of his wardrobe, Yousef proceeded downstairs to find the pool and order a vegetable burger with salad, fries and a large diet coke from the rather limited, poolside bar, daytime menu.

***

Having managed to borrow a metal bowl from the Union Hotel's kitchen, Achmed left the full packet of dried chickpeas soaking beside the beige, imitation marble, wash-hand basin in his bedroom in readiness to be transformed into humus. The search for the other humus ingredients gave him and Noor an opportunity to explore the town and see if there were any clues as to why Yousef had chosen it for a rendezvous. Near to the Sheriff's office was a small row of independent stores. Mabel's Deli and Emporium was a new shop which had opened only a few weeks before and had an excellent range of American and foreign foods along with some small domestic kitchen equipment.

Achmed was surprised and delighted that they had everything he would need to make a perfect humus meal. As the list of ingredients was asked for and one by one placed on the counter and rung up on the new, white, electronic till, a two way conversation started up between Noor and Charlie, the young, chatty, red-haired shop assistant who appeared to be trying to impress her.

Two Lemons: "You all up here, for the shale oil meeting?" asked Charlie.

Three Large heads of Garlic: "My brother and I just wanted a break from the City," replied Noor.

Extra virgin olive oil: "Oh, he's your brother, I thought…."

Pestle and Mortar: "What are all those police doing here?" asked Noor.

Packet of Cumin seeds: "They found a dead body in a new Cadillac. He had been shot through the head. Word is that it was the big oilman who was coming here for the town's Shale oil meeting at the hotel."

Electric blender: "Do they know who did the killing?" asked Noor.

Packet of sea salt: "Sheriff thinks it could be environmentalists, but the State police think it's a local with a grudge."

Tahini: "I like your shop a lot and we will be back. Would you mind telling me if anything else interesting happens while we are staying here?" asked Noor.

Large packet of cracker biscuits: "No Ma'am, sure thing. My name's Charlie and I'm here most days."

Charlie bundled everything into three, large, paper carrier bags emblazoned with the shop's name and helped them to the door.

"One thing is certain; if you want to know what's happening in Molinos Ridge, you don't need the internet, radio or T.V. you just ask Charlie at the Deli," said Noor to Achmed as they walked back to the hotel. They were sound in the knowledge they could eat halal this far away from L.A. and wait in safety for the arrival of Yousef.

CHAPTER 15

Jools checked her watch. I think that's time, she thought, as she wrote down, on her hand-tooled, brown, leather-bound notepad, the phone number of the little terraced house in Belfast that her friend at the T.V. station had emailed to her. 00 44 28…. she began to key.

At the same moment she was dialling on her land line, her cell phone began to ring. It was Alistair.

"Hi, Darling," answered Jools. "No, I wasn't asleep. I'm not even in bed yet. Yes, I'm fine. I was just about to phone Ireland. Remember I told you about it. Yes, I'll tell you if anything interesting comes from my conversation with them. What's that? You think your dad had better taste than that little woman. Very funny! Yeah, yeah, I'll call you later. Love you. Bye."

Jools dialled Belfast again, but this time the full number. The phone rang out for a few seconds that seemed like an age while Brenda, waiting silently and alone for the call, summoned up the courage to pick up and answer.

Jools spoke first.

"Hello, this is Jools McKenzie calling from New Jersey. Who am I speaking to?"

"This is Brenda McConnell in Belfast. You are

speaking to Brenda," was her softly spoken reply.

"Did you get my letter, about your son Daniel?" asked Jools.

"I did indeed," replied Brenda, speaking a little louder because of the distance.

"Mrs. McKenzie, would you mind if I asked you a couple of questions about you and your husband that might explain a few things."

"Sure, fire away," said Jools sipping some Perrier water from a hand-cut, crystal glass she'd taken from the set in the display section of her luxury, custom-built kitchen.

"Was your husband brought up at home as a Roman Catholic?"

"Yes, both his parents are Catholic, as am I, as are both of our sons. I'm sorry to say, but we don't attend chapel very often now that the boys are older. We attend only at Christmas and Easter most years."

Jools had heard about how sectarian Belfast was and wondered if Brenda would have agreed to talk to her, if she had turned out to have been a Protestant.

"What's your husband's birthday and where was he born?"

"26th September, in Edinburgh, Scotland."

"Yes, that would sound about right," answered Brenda before starting her story.

"You need to understand that things were different in those days. My husband was a heavy drinker and after he lost his third job as a used car salesman, well, no one in the car business in this city would give him another chance. One day he left our flat, he went to the railway station and got on a train heading down into the Republic and he just never came back. I already had three young children to feed and was pregnant with twins. When they were born, the little sisters, the nuns, were the only people who would help me. Daniel was first born and completely healthy, but they told me that his brother, born a few minutes later, was very sick. The nuns said he needed a big operation and that I should take Daniel home and they would take care of everything."

Jools listened intently just saying, "O.K.," occasionally as the story unfolded.

"I was home for three days when they sent for me to go back to DeMontford house to see the Mother Superior. She told me my second twin son was going to need medical care for his whole life and I should hand him over to a rich family that they knew who had no children of their own and wanted a child, a boy. They could look after him better than me. I didn't want to do it, believe me, but they convinced me it was best for the baby and for his twin, Daniel, as well as for me and our other children. So I signed a piece of paper in the office, the same day. As God is my witness, I have regretted doing it and leaving him there, every single day of my life.

"And you think Alistair is actually your son?"

"They were identical twins, born on the 21st September. Does your husband have any distinguishing marks on him?"

"Well, there is only one thing I can think of. For quite a young man, Alistair suffers from a severe form of varicose veins. When I first saw them, I described his legs to my best friend as looking like they were raspberry ripple flavour. He isn't in any pain or danger, he just won't go near a pair of shorts or swimming trunks because he is very insecure about how his legs look. His doctor sold him some elastic stockings to wear under his suit, but he refuses to put them on. I don't know why, as I'm the only one who would see them."

"Our Daniel has the same thing. He is exactly the same. He refused point blank to get his legs seen to."

"Does Daniel know he was a twin?" asked Jools, trying to take it all in, conscious of the huge consequences for Alistair and her family from the revelations now coming from Belfast.

"No one knew. I was so ashamed of myself and how selfish I had been that I told everyone at the time Daniel was the only one born alive. After a while we got on with our lives. I met a new man, not the man I'm with just now, you understand, and everything moved forward from there.

"Please tell me, is your husband, my son, a well man?" asked Brenda.

"Apart from the occasional cold etc., I don't think he has ever been anything but really fit his whole life. He played Rugby for his school and was interested in sailing at University. No, he has always been fine," answered Jools, still trying to come to terms with it all.

"He went to University?"

"Yes, St. Andrews. You know the same University that England's Prince William went to, where he met Kate for the first time. Alistair earned a first class degree."

"Is that so," pondered Brenda.

Jools quickly recovered her determined streak and said. "This news, when it gets out, could be devastating for both our families. Alistair will need to know, but he is away from home this week and it's not the kind of thing I want to tell him in a hotel room on his own. Would you mind if we keep this to ourselves, until I can find a way and a time to break it to him gently. I would really appreciate it if we can keep a lid on it until then."

Brenda agreed and said "It's a lot for me to take in as well. I've been trying to find him for years with no luck. Changing his date of birth and registering it in Edinburgh five days later must have been why I hit a brick wall at every turn. Yes, its best we stop and think before we go any further. What those nuns did was… well it was really wicked, you know. I don't want to cause anyone any more trouble."

"Don't worry Brenda. You are not causing anyone any trouble at all. I just need some time to think about how and when I tell him.

Brenda thought carefully then responded, "You can take all the time you need. I'm just grateful he has a lovely wife, like you, to look after him. If there is any chance you have a photo of you and him and your children? Of course, I would really appreciate it if you could post them to me here in my home in Belfast. But mark it private. It's difficult enough to keep any kind of secret in this house at the best of times."

"Oh, and Jools, if I can call you that? There is one other thing I need to tell you. Your husband has a sister, my daughter Mary. She is a good soul, but a poor one at the moment. She is very ill in hospital here in Belfast, and Alistair, as you call him, might be able to help. We were hoping Daniel might turn up again, but that's a bit of a pipe dream right now. So please, I understand that you need to take your time, but if you could act quite quickly it could make all the difference to her right now."

Jools agreed and in addition told Brenda that she would send the photos and asked for some photos in return. Some of Brenda's family were on Facebook and Jools took down every bit of contact information she could think of before ending the conversation.

My God, thought Jools his father and mother are not his real parents and they've lied to him his whole life. He's not even Scottish and he's so very proud of that. He hasn't even been celebrating his birthday on the right day and. Oh shit, Jools rarely, if ever uttered a swear word or even though one. He has a twin brother who is, in all probability, the cold blooded murderer who the English newspapers are calling Jihadi Mick. That's going to go down a treat at our country club and is sure to impress Alistair's fellow executives at the

Company. Oh, and God almighty, what will our boys make of it all. We might have to take them out of school?

Jools decided that complete secrecy was needed until she could decide what to do next.

***

Yousef sat down on one of the red, plastic, 'Coca-Cola' chairs beside the pool bar and began to eat hungrily. It may only be a vegetable burger but to a hungry man it was a feast, thought Yousef. As he sat there in his expensive new Lacoste clothing, he wondered if something was giving away his true identity and purpose. It was the first time in ages that he didn't have a gun with him. It made him feel naked and vulnerable, as if everyone was watching him and passing judgement. He looked at the ordinary cutlery rolled in a white paper napkin and delivered to his table with his meal and, just as he considered what damage he could do to his fellow diners with the knife and fork, it suddenly dawned on him why people were walking away from him and giving him odd looks. Despite washing often, he smelled strongly of fish. He had been sitting in the service boat, which must have been used for fishing before it carried him safely to the nearby jetty. He quickly finished his meal then returned to his room, showering and changing again before going back downstairs to the reception. In a corner of the lobby sat a formal writing desk deliberately placed on its own, sitting on an ornate rug, in the middle of the floor. Seated behind the desk on a secretary-type, swivel chair was a short fat Thomson holiday rep. Yousef thought she had a face like a bat. She was dressed in her distinctive livery of blue skirt and canary yellow blouse topped off with a colourful scarf and finally a pair of wide, dark blue, court shoes. Her name tag said 'Gina'.

"May I sit down?" Yousef asked, as he pulled one of the three, upright, blue velvet covered, silver metal chairs towards him.

"How can I help you?" asked Gina, with one eye on Yousef while the other scanned her laptop, which was switched on and open in front of her.

"I nearly always travel with Thomson, but not on this trip," said Yousef. "I wonder if you could help me."

"I will do what I can," replied Gina as she counted her welcome meeting invites silently through her hands.

"I've just had some bad news from home."

"I'm sorry to hear that," replied Gina, working hard on her smile and trying her best to look like she meant it.

"Yes, I need to return home to Dublin right away and I wondered if you might have a ticket for a seat on one of your planes, that I could buy."

"Normally, we are fully booked, but you may just be in luck. We have an Irish family of three who have to stay on, as their son was injured in the pool of this hotel yesterday. And now they can't travel back to Dublin for at least another four days. I'll just check for you and see when the flight departs." Gina looked through her folder until she found the correct page.

"15.40 hours tomorrow. The coach leaves this hotel at 09.30. Will I see if there is still a seat available on it, for you?"

"Yes please," responded Yousef, who was wondering in his mind, where he could ditch his two pistols before travelling to the airport the next morning.

"I just emailed and got a reply from our office. If you want to go, you would need to pay me right now, in full. It's 368 euros including taxes and transfer. If that's O.K. for you, how would you like to pay?"

"I still have cash left. I wasn't expecting to stay such a short time in Cyprus. Would cash be okay?"

"Yes, I can take cash," responded Gina as she counted the money Yousef handed to her and carefully zipped it into a blue plastic purse then placed her purse back into her briefcase. "This is your receipt for the cash. I will have your ticket and printed boarding pass with me when I come with the coach tomorrow. Do you have your passport on you? I will just need to get a photocopy of it for our records. You are allowed only one suitcase of up to twenty kilos and one cabin bag of no more than five kilos. Put anything sharp or liquid in your hold case and don't be late tomorrow as we won't wait for you or give refunds at this late stage. Okay then, see you at 09.30 tomorrow." Gina closed her laptop and signalled to a badly sunburned elderly couple to approach her desk as Yousef stood up and headed out into the hotel's colourful, tropical gardens.

As he walked through the wrought-iron gate and along the pretty lane that led down to the town, he passed a kiosk selling ice lollies, cans of coke, bottled water, crisps, paperback novels and a few English newspapers, placed, with their headlines showing outwards, on a tall revolving metal stand. On the stand was an 'overseas edition' copy of 'The Sun' priced at 4 euros. It was covered in headlines about how the Americans believed they had killed the infamous 'Jihadi Mick' in a drone strike, North of Aleppo in Syria. Silly bastards, thought Yousef. Soon they will know the taste of their own blood. I'm going to bite the head off that Satan they call America. Soon they will all know my real name. With that thought leaving his mind and images of the sweltering heat of area 51 entering it, Yousef ordered one of the P and P, strawberry and chocolate, grand cone's that were advertised on the big aluminium poster on the side of the kiosk and walked on towards the town, looking for a bin big enough for him to drop the two pistols into. The guns had served their purpose and he now had them well concealed on him. They were wrapped in a hotel pillow case that he'd taken from the cleaner's linen cart while it was left unattended for a moment, parked in the hall outside the room in front of his.

Checking no one was looking, he casually tossed the pillowcase, and the half eaten ice cream cone into a large, metal roadside bin and headed into the town. Soon it would be time to pray again and once again Yousef had much to be thankful for.

CHAPTER 16

Alistair skipped his favourite full hotel breakfast. He'd woken early using an alarm and he'd hastily eaten scrambled egg off some plain white crockery, which was placed on a big, plastic, room service tray and had been delivered with a polite knock on his door. To save him time in the morning, he had visited the reception and booked his breakfast tray the night before. He then arranged to pay his meals and accommodation invoice, in full, with his Company Credit card and effectively checked out, but without vacating his room or returning his electronic keys. In any case, Alistair would be eating again in around an hour and a half when he took part in the launch party at Manor Motors. They had selected to hold an early morning special event for the new model to try to snag a load of potential customers when they drove their kids to the nearby schools. The general idea was that these potential customers could be drawn into the dealership by the promise of some free hot food and competition prizes, along with a free car wash and vacuum and a current valuation of their existing cars. Alistair believed it was a good idea, but it was also the reason he had to dash into the countryside to catch a small, single-engine plane, up to Carson City later that day, The 'Manor Motors gig', as he put it, had made a big hole in an otherwise, quite civilised schedule.

The breakfast launch event ran very well. There were enough potential customers gorging on food and taking part in competitions which gathered their names, contact details and current car values, to warrant his visit and the costs of the catering and the promotion. Once again, the garage owners had included a Scottish element to the proceedings. As the customers gathered at the front of the covered up new car, just before the reveal and starting the offer of breakfast, the garage owner took the microphone and began to sing 'Auld Lang Syne', using a mock Scottish accent and intended to be in Alistair's honour. At the same moment the song's well known lyrics left the man's lips, 'Should auld acquaintance be forgot and never come to mind', the transatlantic, fibre optic, phone cable between the United States and the United Kingdom which carried the digital imprint of the voices of Jools and Brenda McConnell, had already done the exact opposite of the sentiment of the world famous, Robert Burns song. What was being uncovered and remembered and brought to mind was wiping out Alistair's Scottish roots, his own personal history and a big chunk of who he considered himself to be.

***

Yousef enjoyed listening to the waves crashing and foaming onto the shore, the twinkling of the stars, and the slight smell of seaweed in the air as he got nearer to the water's edge. After the dryness of Syria and the madness of the boat trip, just standing quietly watching the waves was enough for him at that moment.

The only annoyance was that further down the

beach, some teenagers had started a fire with a few lumps of driftwood and were dancing on the sand to the sound of a guitar. They were all probably drunk as well he thought, as he considered how handy a machine gun or a grenade would have been in his hands, at that precise moment.

He decided to silently creep up on them. Firstly, because he could, but also because he wanted to look at the girls, who seemed to be wearing very little and who were leaping about dancing under the moonlight and moving around on the golden sand with bare feet, while surrounded by the sweet, smoky smell of the dry driftwood, burning and crackling. In the flickering light of the fire, Yousef, a seasoned soldier, recognised a familiar pattern. Two of the young guys were separating out one particular girl, who looked a bit younger than the rest and drawing her away from the herd, much in the way a big cat would single out the weakest wildebeest at a watering hole. He looked closely at this girl who he could now see quite clearly. There was something about her that reminded him of his own sister Mary, back in Belfast. She was the one who'd looked after him at school when the other kids had been cruel about his learning difficulty and his missing father.

Over a period of time the boys managed to entice the girl away from the fire and closer to where Yousef was hiding. Just far enough away from the crowd to conceal what they had in mind. Yousef looked on as one of the boys stood behind her and held a small pocket knife to the girl's throat while his friend stood in front and unzipped her shorts, dropped them to the ground, pushed his hand down into the front of her underpants, and pressed his face against hers.

"Just what do you think you're doing," bellowed Yousef at the top of his voice. The two boys looked, turned then ran down the beach, through the foaming water, away from the party and away from Yousef and the girl. "Are you okay?" asked Yousef.

"I am now," replied the girl, hastily pulling up and zipping her figure hugging, light blue, denim shorts and looking around for her shoulder bag.

"Are you staying at this hotel? Would you like me to walk you home? I don't think those guys will come back, but, you never know," said Yousef, in his most gentle voice.

"Thank you very much, that would be really great; you've saved me. Please don't tell my parents, what happened here tonight. They warned me, but I just didn't listen. I'll be in terrible trouble if they find out that I was nearly… well you know what they were going to do to me."

"I can guess. I'll walk you back to the hotel, I'm staying there too and I won't tell your parents what has happened, on one condition." The girl looked at him and began to become worried again.

"What's the condition?" she asked nervously.

"The condition is that you tell them yourself, tonight. Trust me. It will be for the best."

Yousef left the girl in the safety of the reception.

Then he asked for his key and took the lift upstairs to his room to get ready for his early start and his coach trip with all the other tourists, going to the airport the next morning. Within an hour there was a knock on his bedroom door. He was a bit apprehensive and, holding a glass bottle out of sight to use as a weapon, cautiously opened the door. In front of him was an English couple in their early fifties, nicely dressed for the evening and standing a little nervously in front of his door. The woman spoke first.

"I believe we are very much in your debt," she said, starting to gain more confidence. "It was our daughter Patty, who you saved from the gang of boys tonight." Patty had obviously changed the story a little to avoid the wrath of her family and in doing so had made Yousef out to be a bigger hero than he actually was. "Patty told us everything. How you risked your life and fought them off with only a big stick. I don't know how we can ever thank you. Can we start by giving you this bottle of whisky? You must need a drink after an ordeal like that?" asked Patty's father.

"No thanks, you see, I don't drink. I'm a strict Muslim and never drink alcohol. I was just preparing for my prayers before retiring to my bed, but please, do come in for a moment."

The two stood rather uncomfortably in Yousef's bedroom. Patty's father spoke first. "Well you know I haven't always spoken kindly about people of your religion. All those extremists on the television tend to colour your view of the world. But, after the way you behaved tonight, I can promise you that I will never say or even think another bad thing about your people ever again. I swear it."

"That's very good of you," responded Yousef, while thinking to himself, I wish these two idiots would leave now and take their stinking bottle of alcohol with them.

"If I can't give you a gift, is there anything else I can do for you?" asked the man.

"Well there are two things. I have to return home tomorrow without delay, so please keep the authorities out of this until I'm gone." The man agreed.

"And the other thing?" asked the man.

"Please ask Patty to dress in a more modest way. Her dress code attracts the wrong type of attention and I believe this was probably the cause of what happened tonight. You wouldn't find a Muslim girl dressed like that, ever," said Yousef looking at the man sternly and straight in the eye.

"I think she has learned her lesson on that score, but we'll make sure she knows your views as well. She really thinks you were brilliant and hopefully she'll listen to reason this time," replied Patty's mother.

Yousef closed the door as the pair left. He hoped the couple would keep their word. His mission to America was far more important in heaven and earth than the three stupid lives he had just come into contact with and hoped he would never see again.

**

"Miss Rose! Miss Rose! Deputy Sheriff!" Charlie called from the doorway of the Deli, as Rose stood looking at white ribbons and lace in the sunlight outside the Molinos Ridge sewing and haberdashery store.

"Yes Charlie, what crimes have you committed today?" she asked, trying not to laugh at him as he stood in front of her with half a small carton of yoghurt down the front of his T shirt.

"I'm sorry about my appearance Ma'am. I just had a little accident when I was stocking up the refrigerator. It's about the murder. I have a couple of prime suspects for you."

"Go on," said Rose trying not to appear too disinterested. Charlie had a habit of getting involved in all the town's gossip and adding his own special twist to the story which was usually no more than a total figment of his imagination.

"Well I heard that the dead oilman you found was a Jew. Was that right?"

"Might have been," answered Rose.

"Well not long after you found the body, I served two strangers in the shop and they could have been Arabs. They said they were brother and sister, but they're both staying together at the Union Hotel. The clerk at the hotel told me that they arrived, right on cue, holding a shooting bag."

"Were they carrying a rifle?" asked Rose, starting to take an interest.

"No, but they bought some very strange stuff when they came over here."

"What kind of stuff?" asked Rose.

"They bought a blender, some cumin seeds and some stuff that I never sold before called tahini. Do you think they were going to make up a bomb with all that stuff Miss Rose?"

"Charlie, do you not know what tahini is?"

"No, Ma'am, I don't," replied Charlie, starting to realise that he was out on a limb on this one.

"It's an edible paste made using crushed sesame seeds. Heck, Charlie, you're the guy working in the Deli store, and even I knew that. Now, to answer your question, yes, the oilman was Jewish. Although why a group of desperate Arab killers would come all the way out here to kill Jews, when they could have their pick of half the population of Los Angeles, I really don't know. As for constructing a giant tahini bomb. Well it might work if their intended victim had a severe seed allergy; otherwise you should advise them, next time they are in your shop, to head down to the hardware store at the end of this road and go buy some dynamite like everyone else. Honestly Charlie, you're getting worse. Stick to your day job and leave the detective work to me and my brother."

Rose walked back along the road to the sheriff's building and up the broad steps to where her brother was waiting. He was chewing gum and standing with one foot on the low fence post and his hand resting on his father's old Colt pistol which was safely in its holster and strapped by his side.

"What's gottin into you li'l Sis," asked Carlton.

"Men, stupid men!" exclaimed Rose.

"If you're talking about Charlie, he really doesn't qualify. I don't think he's ever had a girlfriend and round here that qualifies him only as a boy. What did he want anyway?"

Rose slapped the side of her head gently then brushed her hair back from her face. "He seems to think we should be looking for a couple of Jew-hating Arabs. He says that we should look at a couple of tourists who just arrived at the hotel who might be sporting a suspicious suntan and eating dangerously."

"Well, you know Rose that just might not be such a bad idea. After all, we don't have any other leads to go on and until S.O.C and forensics tells us more about the bullets that were used we might as well waste our time around the hotel as anywhere else, especially on a nice day like this."

"Sheriff Carlton Culzean," she always used his full name and title when she was annoyed with him, which was quite often. "You may have time to waste, but I certainly don't. We have a murder to solve, so I'm going to get the big blackboard on wheels, which had been set up for the meeting, and bring it over here to the sheriff station. I'll drag it up the invalid's ramp and right into the hallway, on my own if I have to, set it up as a case board and cover it in photographs, information and evidence, just like I was taught to do by the real detectives back in the city."

"Would you like me to lend you a hand with that?" asked Carlton, making a low bowing movement as he spoke.

"Sure would, that is if you're really not doing anything else."

"I'd still like to talk to that couple of strangers. Maybe once I've finished my job as your personal removals man."

"Yeah, yeah, very funny," answered Rose as they walked towards the hotel with Rose in front and Carlton trailing behind.

CHAPTER 17

Yousef decided to get up early and have his breakfast away from the hotel in a small beachside café. He really didn't want to get involved with the over-grateful family from the night before. There were just enough times that he could hear the words, 'your people,' without taking something hard and smashing it over the girl's father's head.

He sipped away at what, on first impression, looked like a bottle of Scottish Highland spring water. The prominent label proudly called it 'High lander'. After studying the blue and white label, at the back of the bottle, he found that it came from a local company called Farmakas. Every drop was from Cyprus and it had never been near Scotland in its life. It is really nice water, thought Yousef, who sat overlooking the beach in the blinding morning sunshine wearing a newly acquired pair of black, plastic framed sunglasses. He relaxed contemplating and comparing his life to the plastic bottle he held in his hand. I didn't start life as a Muslim, just like this water didn't start life as Scottish. But I am a Muslim. One of the best Muslims, who would gladly give his life and take life for Allah and for all Muslims who are threatened in our own lands. He undid a button and pulled his current passport from the back pocket of his expensive Lacoste trousers. He rubbed the document against the leg of the table to weather it before it went on display at its most important outing yet, namely at the departure desks of L.C.A. Larnaca International Airport.

Patrick Murphy, I wonder how they came up with a clever name like that? Surely there must be a more Irish name I could have used for my new Irish passport? Well Patrick, you're almost famous. After that stupid girl has finished telling her story you'll sound like you're a one man army. It was easy to fool the hotel receptionist with the passport, especially as the matching credit card actually worked. It could be a different matter at an airport with all the scanners and everything, thought Yousef as he committed to his memory the date and place of birth plus the home address and phone number for Patrick, in case he got taken aside and questioned.

***

"Mrs. Bernstein, if you would like to have a seat in this office, my brother, Sheriff Culzean, will be with you in a moment. Can I get you a coffee?"

"Thank you, my dear, you've been very kind," replied the slim, well-dressed, attractive, dark haired lady, who's oilman husband had been found shot dead on his way to the town's meeting.

Carlton entered the room.

"Mrs. Bernstein, this is my brother, our Sheriff, who would like to ask you a few routine questions. Would you like me to stay while he takes you through them?" asked Rose gently and sympathetically.

"If you don't mind, my dear. You see its all come as something of a shock."

"Mrs. Bernstein, firstly, please accept on behalf of our town, our deepest sympathy. The questions I am going to ask might seem blunt and very personal, when you are newly grieving, and I apologise in advance for them. I mean you no disrespect. We all just want to get to the truth about what happened.

"Mrs Bernstein, Do you have any idea who might have done this to Mr. Bernstein?"

"His name was Howard."

"Sorry, did Howard have any enemies or anyone you can think of, who would want to do something like this?"

"Howard was great at his job, but what with this fracking thing, he'd upset a few people, but never to this extent."

"And what about your relationship? Was there any friction between you?"

"We've had a wonderful marriage for thirty two years. We have two great kids. My son Ethan is a surgeon and my daughter Rebecca is expecting our first grandchild in three months. She doesn't know yet. How can I tell her?"

At this point Mrs Bernstein's voice faltered and she finally gave in to the tears that she'd kept welled up inside her. She'd been told the dreadful news on the doorstep of her home in the early hours of the morning by a tired, twenty-six year old, African American police woman, soaked through, from a sudden localised thunderstorm.

Carlton decided to end the interview at this point. Heck, the city cops with their guidelines and standards would have kept going for another hour, he thought, but it was obvious to him that this dignified lady had nothing whatsoever to do with her husband's death. Carlton believed he was too experienced and too much of a gentleman to put her through any more hell than she'd already been through in the last few hours.

"Rose, would you take Mrs. Bernstein over to the hotel and look after her? Perhaps you could find her son's phone number and get him up here to look after his Mom. She must be exhausted, what with the travelling and all. Heaven only knows how she got this far on her own?"

"A powerful combination of love and determination," replied Rose, putting her arm around the lady and guiding her out of the office.

"That's about the size of it," said Carlton.

***

Jools found herself, very unusually, in a complete mess. Normally, she and Alistair were at different stages in their emotions. When he was stressed and under any kind of pressure, Jools provided him with everything he could need to get through it. Likewise, Alistair was Jools's anchor in a storm and she really appreciated his unusual ability to become detached from his emotions and deal with things by looking them straight in the eye. But this was different. It was about Alistair, his family and his roots. Who could she turn to for advice?

The story had made her seethe with anger at the Church. Whatever their reasons, this was, in her opinion, completely wrong; a wilful and cruel act to deceive that simple woman and separate two boys who should have supported each other throughout their lives. Still, if things had been different, Jools would never have met Alistair and her two beloved sons would not exist. Perhaps it was God's will, after all. Jools and Alistair were members of the local Roman Catholic Church which was close to their home and affiliated to her boys' school. They regularly paid into the Church funds, but only ever visited in person very occasionally. She actually knew the people at St. Stevens, in Elisabeth, much better than in her own parish as the church website for St. Stevens carried a paid for advert for her real estate company. She had received many listings through their recommendation often following a bereavement, when the family of the deceased found themselves having to put their late relative's property onto the market and needed some impartial advice.

Jools preferred Fr. Anthony to Fr. David who was old, a little deaf and very set in his ways. Perhaps Fr. Anthony could help her to decide what to do next? Jools phoned the rectory using the number printed on her latest advertising receipt and felt a sense of relief when she was given an appointment for a one to one meeting on the same day.

***

Manor Motors gave Alistair the use of a 2010, third generation, red, Ford Ranger pick-up to go on the next leg of his journey, out into the countryside and up to where Mr. Nordstrom was waiting for him, with his Beechcraft, single engine plane. The car had recently been taken as a trade in and had enough small scratches and dents to be handed over without Alistair having to worry about bringing it back looking like a new car. The valeting department had just finished cleaning out the driver's cab for him when Alistair was handed the Ranger's large clump of keys attached to a heavy, horse shoe shaped key ring.

"What's she like?" he asked the young guy who had just finished working the vacuum on the rubber mats from the cab floor.

"You'll be fine with this one; runs real sweet. It's got the four litre V6, so it can really pull."

Alistair, now reassured about his borrowed transport, decided to change into a pair of jeans and a casual shirt to drive the pickup. His suit neatly folded into his case, he set up his satnav and then checked the oil, water and fuel in the car. He then put on his recently purchased pair of Ray Ban Clubmaster, polar special sunglasses and headed north for his rendezvous with Jed up at the airstrip.

***

Achmed was leaning into the trunk of his white Chevrolet in the front of the big parking lot when Sheriff Culzean quietly walked up behind him. Achmed was aware of someone standing behind him and immediately noticed out of the corner of his eye, the shiny, black leather ankle boots and distinctive grey trousers with a broad dark red stripe down the side.

"Enjoying your holiday?" asked Carlton.

"So far. We've not long arrived," replied Achmed, remaining calm and leaving the trunk wide open to avoid any suspicion. He was grateful that the guns were out of sight, covered by a red and blue tartan coloured travelling rug of a type that their employer kept in all of his cars.

"What brings you to these parts? It's not much of a place for a holiday at this time of year."

Achmed had a well-rehearsed answer prepared in case they were asked. "We work in L.A. and the smog is bad for my health. A few days in the mountains will help me recover and get back to work."

"Well there's certainly plenty of good healthy air out here although some people say there is a slight smell of sulphur left over from the old factory, but I've never noticed it. You only need to look at how many old people we have in this town as testament to our healthy environment. Speaking about the environment, you don't happen to know anything about fracking for gas do you?"

"Sorry, not a thing," replied Achmed.

"I don't suppose you've heard of a man called Bernstein?" quizzed Carlton.

"Only, that he's dead. They told me about it at the hotel reception," responded Achmed, raising his eyebrows and trying to act detached from the question.

"Well don't let that put you off your holiday.

We've got a great little town here. We normally never get anything like this happening. In fact, statistically, it's one of the safest places to live in America."

"I'm not worried at all. In fact, we would feel safer on the deck of the Titanic staring down an iceberg, than being back in crazy L.A. The safety aspect is one of the things we love most about this area," replied Achmed, smiling.

"Yep, I bet it is. My sister Rose worked as a cop in L.A. She could tell you some stories that would make your hair curl. Well, anyway, I won't keep you any longer. I hope you and your sister have a nice, safe stay in our town. Remember your sheriff is here for you, if you need me."

Carlton put a piece of his favourite cinnamon chewing gum in his mouth and headed into the hotel bar for his usual complementary, big glass of diet coke with ice and lemon.

**

Jools took the phone call from St. Steven's on her cell phone, using the Bluetooth hands free in her Porsche, while on the way to her meeting with Father Anthony.

"Yes, Mrs. McKenzie. I thought I would save you from a wasted journey. I've talked it over with our Bishop who was honouring us with a personal visit today. Even though we know you, this is not your parish. Your family are not even members of our Diocese. The Bishop has told me, and I agree with him, that it would be better for all concerned, if you raise such matters with your local priest who is best placed to help you on an on-going basis. I'm sorry I couldn't be of more help to you."

"Okay, thanks for your call. I will make the arrangements. Goodbye," said Jools. She was thinking when she heard the news, they were quick enough to take her money and free professional advice, funny how everything changes when she needed their help. They probably smelled a whiff of scandal, which there is in this case, and decided to sidestep it off to someone else.

She decided that the best way for her to deal with this, from now on, was on her own. The next phone call was to her in-laws in Scotland to get their side of the story.

CHAPTER 18

The last few hundred yards towards the airstrip was more of a rutted track than an actual road and Alistair was grateful that Manor Motors had lent him a vehicle with a good ground clearance. As the car bounced the last few yards towards the automated security gate, he could see evidence of where money had been spent. A brand new aircraft sat on a smooth concrete pad. The long, straight runway was well constructed using level tarmac. A broken white line ran along its entire centre and there were modern landing lights placed at regular intervals along both sides. Beside a white painted trailer tank with the words 'Aviation fuel. Highly flammable,' neatly hand-painted in red on its sides, was a wooden structure resembling a log cabin. It had a fifty foot high, aerial mast, clamped securely with steel brackets, to the stone-ended wall which included the little building's traditional chimney.

Alistair pulled up beside an identical car to the one he was driving; same model and same colour. He was glad to open the car door, stretch out his tired legs and get some fresh air into his lungs.

"I like your choice of cars," said the owner as he outstretched his hand in welcome.

"You must be Jed," said Alistair.

"And you must be Mr. McKenzie," came the

reply. "Funny, after talking to your assistant in New York, I was expecting a man in a business suit driving a big flash car."

"Yes, I gave him the day off today," joked Alistair.

Jed's bulging black flight bag sat on the counter waiting to be carried onto the aircraft. "I understand that you're also a pilot?" enquired Jed.

"I've had my license for a number of years. I learned to fly at Prestwick airport in Scotland. You fly out straight above the sea and it can get really windy there, especially when landing," responded Alistair.

Jed's reply surprised Alistair. "Yes, I've been to Prestwick in Scotland often and it can get very windy there. It was our first stop across the Atlantic on the way to our German bases during the cold war. I was an Air Force pilot for eighteen years before I went into semi-retirement here in the mountains. I won't need your assistance today, but it's always nice to have someone qualified, riding shotgun, on my new Beech."

"I don't suppose you were the one who flew Elvis Presley to Prestwick Airport when he was doing his National Service?" asked Alistair.

"That was a bit before my time. I was there from the mid-eighties to 2003. I would have liked to though. I was always a big fan of the king," replied Jed. "I don't remember there being a flying school operating out of Prestwick."

"There wasn't," replied Alistair. "My dad kept a single engine private plane of his own at the airport and his yacht a couple of miles away in a place called Troon."

"Sounds like you had a nice start in life."

"It sure was," replied Alistair.

The speed of take-off and the rate of climb of this new model plane really impressed Alistair.

"I've got some coffee in that flask behind you. It's got full cream milk but no sugar, as I'm type two diabetic and don't do so much sugar any more. There are some peanut cluster cookies in a box beside the coffee flask if you want something sweet. I just thought, I hope you're not allergic to peanuts or anything. We offer a first class service to our clients. I call it the best in the west."

"So I believe," replied Alistair helping himself to a cookie.

Landing a small aircraft at a busy large airport like Carson City didn't seem to bother Jed. His familiarity with the route, and his years in the Air Force, had given him a natural authority when talking to air traffic control and finding his way over to where all the other small, light planes were parked. As they pulled up to a stop, Alistair could see a great big man leaning on the open driver's door of a brand new, top of the range, white Lincoln Sedan. Big Jim perhaps, thought Alistair. He certainly was big at almost seven foot tall and over 280lbs in weight.

***

In the reception of his hotel, Yousef stood with the other guests who had checked out that morning and were awaiting the arrival of various holiday companies providing coach and minibus transport to the airport. They could be distinguished from other guests moving through the lobby by the sweaters and heavy coats hanging over their suitcases, in anticipation of leaving the heat of Cyprus behind for another year. As each bus drew up, guests checked to see if it was for them. Around 9.45, the light blue Kapnos and Sons bus with 'Thompson Holidays' and 'coach 4' showing on a card in the front window, finally arrived. No bat faced girl, thought Yousef, concerned about his boarding pass. The driver reversed the bus towards the entrance door and walked into the reception shouting, "Murphy, Kirios (the Greek word for mister) Murphy." Two families and Yousef came forward, but it turned out that the envelope the driver carried was for Yousef and contained his boarding pass and a printed receipt.

Yousef made a point of being chatty going onto the bus. Asking his fellow passengers if they had enjoyed their holiday and whereabouts they lived back in Ireland. One woman called Sheila was travelling alone with two small children. Within a few moments, he had her whole life story. How she worked as an administrator in a mashed potato factory near Oldcastle. How her husband had left her and that her holiday had been good but a bit lonely. Yousef decided that Sheila and her kids would provide a good cover for him going through the airport security and decided to turn his charm levels up to maximum and stick close to her and her noisy children. Getting off the bus, the driver laid out all the cases along the pavement at the airport's 'Departures' entrance. Yousef immediately offered to get a trolley and put all the cases including his own onto it. He then asked if she or the children were hungry and would they like a drink, as it was a long flight and they'd probably need something. Sheila found the nearest bar and ordered a beer and soft drinks and asked if Yousef would like a beer.

"I would prefer some water but let me pay for this," he said, trying not to breath in the smell of beer from the tray which he ended up carrying to the table.

***

Jools made another cup of coffee and kept an eye on her gold Rolex Datejust, diamond watch. She was never very good at working out the time difference between New Jersey and Scotland. All she knew was that the late afternoon was best as Edinburgh was six hours behind them and she wanted to catch Alistair's mother at home around the time she started to make her breakfast.

"Yes dear, it's lovely to talk to you too. Are you all well? How are Alistair and the kids?" Jools had some serious questions to ask but was finding it hard to find the words. At last she hit on a plan to get things started.

"Alistair's fine but the Company is paying for him to have a complete body scan and a top of the line preventative health check. They're doing it for all the senior executives. He will need to know a lot more detail about his family's health history. He has a six page form for the Company doctors. As it seems to matter a lot to them would you be able to help me fill it in?"

Alistair's mother was a retired lawyer and still as sharp as the day she left court for the last time. There was a long silence before she asked,

"Have you heard something?" was her carefully chosen response.

"I've been speaking to someone in Ireland," replied Jools.

"My gosh, I always knew this day might come. What has been said? How much do you know?"

"Quite possibly a lot more than even you do," replied Jools, hoping the shock of the past re-emerging would not kill the old lady, strong though she was.

Jools told almost the whole story as she had heard it and Mrs McKenzie was able to confirm most of it. They had been unable to have a child. Alistair's adoptive father was a major financial contributor to a number of Roman Catholic charities in Glasgow, Edinburgh and Belfast where he had offices. When they were contacted about a healthy baby in need of a home they jumped at the chance and the option to register his birth in Edinburgh a couple of days later, simply managed to make everything less complicated. It seemed only natural to the couple to bring him up unaware of his start.

"After all, on paper as well as at home, he was always our son and we gave him everything a boy could wish for."

When Jools told her that Alistair was born a twin, the old lady said that she was profoundly shocked and, if they'd known that, they would have gladly taken them both.

"How could they do something like that to a little boy and to us?" Mrs McKenzie, now gently sobbing into a Kleenex as she held the phone with her hand trembling asked. "Is his twin still alive, could he and his mother want to meet Alistair?" she asked innocently.

Jools decided to spare her mother-in-law any additional trauma by saying, "We think he's abroad and can't be contacted right now. And the Irish woman really doesn't know what to do and has asked me to sit on the information until she does."

Mrs McKenzie agreed and pleaded with Jools not to tell Alistair right away.

"Not until we have all had a chance to think."

Jools replied that this had also been her first reaction and was happy to go along with that plan for now.

**

Big Jim smelled strongly of Aramis aftershave and his car had the equally strong aroma of his favourite imported Stradavarius cigars. The combination of the two was making Alistair feel a bit queasy in a way that the journey in a light plane through the mountains should have, but didn't.

"Do you mind if I open a window?" he asked.

"No, you go right ahead and soak up some of that pure Carson City air, Son. It will build you up an appetitive for what we have planned for you later today after our launch."

"Yes Bernice, my P.A., mentioned something

about a special meal you had arranged for me; that was very kind of you."

"Think nothing of it; it's just a bit of money and what's that compared to you having to hire a plane just to visit us. Tonight you are going to experience the meal of your life!"

"What, do they kill you after you've eaten?" joked Alistair.

"No son, that's what they call a unique and amazing experience at a very special restaurant. It's the dandiest thing you've ever tried. We think you'll love it. Just don't eat too much at our launch. That normal food is just for the public. You get yourself away from the garage as early as is respectable and come with me to the Little Amsterdam restaurant. Yes sir, you are in for a treat, a real treat that you can tell all the folks back in New York about. Just a pity your wife couldn't join us; perhaps next time."

"Yes, perhaps," said Alistair, trying hard not to appear too sceptical.

***

Yousef decided to take a proper look at Sheila and the kids. Yes, he thought, we could look like a family returning from holiday, even if Sheila did look like she was 'built for comfort rather than speed'.

Before long and after he had bought a few more drinks and food for her and sweets that the kids wanted, Sheila gave Yousef her phone number and address. He returned the compliment by giving her his false name, address and the phone number he had memorised over breakfast at the beach.

Although they were seated at opposite ends of the aircraft, Yousef dutifully visited Sheila often. On one occasion he bought and delivered to her a copy of 'the despised', Hello magazine and later some prize scratch cards. His personal abhorrence of gambling was less significant than his desire to ingratiate himself. He was trying hard at being a perfect find for her to tell all her stupid, Godless friends at the factory about, when she got back to work on Monday. All the effort was so, when he approached the perspex and aluminium box containing the border guards at the EU Passport control entry point at Dublin Airport, he would look like part of one of those modern Irish families with parents having different surnames, returning from a week in the sun with Thomson's package holidays. Only he knew he was a cold blooded Jihadi murderer on his way to stock up with more cash and documents before going on to take Jihad to the heart of the great Satan, Area 51, U.S.A.

CHAPTER 19

Brenda had summoned all her immediate family for an important meeting which included her children as well as her best friend Janice, from across the street. When they all finally arrived they spread throughout her small terraced house. Brenda drew everyone's attention by hitting a spoon against an empty Guinness glass a few times until the house fell silent as everyone gathered in the kitchen.

"My dear friend Janice and my family, I've asked you all here today to tell you a secret. Now I don't want any of this to go beyond my house and, if it does, I'll know that one of you has blabbed. It's an important secret."

"Is it about my dad?" asked one of her older sons.

"The only secret about your dad was that he was a feckin idiot and that wasn't much of a secret to anyone. In fact, it turned out that I was the last one to know. Fortunately, you took after me and not him, or you'd be a useless Dublin piss artist, the same as he is."

"Is it about Daniel, cause if it is, we already know he murders people in Arabia." said another, smaller, boy.

"Strangely enough, no, it is not about Daniel, or

Yousef as he likes to call himself now, although he is involved in what I have to talk to you about. No, it's about me.

"Apart from Daniel and Mary, is every one of my children here?" asked Brenda, as she quizzically looked each of them straight in the eye.

They looked around the cramped room at each other and answered, "Yes," in harmony.

"Well you would all be wrong. You see Alistair's missing."

"Who the feck is Alistair," quickly asked one of her children.

Janice, Benda's oldest friend had been told the full story, in between tears, very soon after her transatlantic conversation with Jools had finished. The rest of the family listened, open mouthed, occasionally throwing in questions like, "Is he going to stay here?" "What's he like?" and "Is he rich?" By the end of the evening, the mood had changed to, "It wasn't your fault Mammy," and "He missed out on a great start," and "Those bastard nuns want stringing up."

Brenda thanked her family for their support and reminded them of their promise to keep it all quiet for now. On the subject of the nuns, she said, "I don't want any of that type of talk. This is a respectable house and we need to agree that whatever the rights and wrongs of this may have been, it was all a long time ago. Heck, most of those nuns will be dead by now and it will be more than just us, who will be judging them."

***

Alistair found Big Jim's office really interesting. As well as the framed, blue football shirt and signed photo from the local boys' soccer club, which the garage had sponsored for the last three seasons, Big Jim kept a tall, steel and glass case with a lot of old motoring memorabilia, including a small collection of vintage car mascots and badges. Included in the collection was a tall, Rolls Royce Flying Lady, signed by the original artist and an almost priceless French Lalique mascot that once adorned the radiator cap on a 1920's Hispano Suiza.

"Used to belong to a famous French Count," said Big Jim. "My Dad bought it in an antique auction in Paris in the sixties when he went there to visit the Louvre museum. Over here is one from my own personal collection, take a look." Big Jim handed Alistair a heavy, highly polished, mahogany plaque with thirty, nineteenth century, silver dollars carefully sunk into it and the letters C.C. embossed in silver at the top. "Take a guess at what this set is worth?"

Alistair thinking $50 a piece for the silver dollars plus another $60 for the plaque answered, "Around $1600."

Jim laughed, shook his head and said, "Look a bit closer. Each of these coins was made in the late 1800's and they were minted right here in Carson City. I've looked all over the United States and up into Canada and even Mexico to build up that collection. The insurance value is over $500 for each coin, making the whole lot worth around ten times more than you thought at over $16,000 in total. Just a tip, when you are back in New York. If you should find a silver dollar with the letters C.C. written real small on it, you buy it and call me right away. There will be cash waiting here for you, all day long."

***

Despite the inevitable baby crying only a few feet away from him, and the lack of any leg room causing stiffness and irritation in his long legs, Yousef managed to get a bit of sleep for the last hour of his holiday flight into Dublin. Looking out of the window, he could already see the big difference in the weather between Larnaca and Dublin. Still, at least his clothes were consistent with someone who had become accustomed to the holiday sun for a few days and forgotten about the weather at home he thought. As he sized up the crew's attitude towards him he wondered if they were about to alert the authorities on the ground that the infamous 'Jihadi Mick' was on board. Then remembering that 'Jihadi Mick' was meant to be dead, he gained a little confidence and looked back down the plane to where Sheila was sitting, giving her a last playful wave before the crew took their seats for landing.

Dublin Airport was much larger and more modern than he'd remembered it and he tried not to look too interested in the huge, silver coloured building. After all, he was supposed to have only left from it a few days before. The walk from the baggage collection area towards passport control was a long one and took ages. As they approached the customs officer, both Sheila and Yousef presented their own passports and the kid's passports together. Then, after a cursory glance and without a word spoken, the four passports were returned to them and they walked out of the secure area together. Keeping up the pretence, 'gentleman' Yousef helped Sheila control the excited children as they collected their luggage. They then passed through the green, nothing to declare route, out of the customs hall and into the airport concourse. Yousef couldn't wait to ditch Sheila and the kids. After a quick peck on her cheek and a "please keep in touch," he was into his laptop for an expensive, above suspicion, hotel room for a night or two and a quick email to his contacts for a meeting, as soon as it could be arranged. It was a day too late to use the airport hotel booking Mohammed had arranged for him while in Syria. He then checked out the airport shopping parade for the Hugo Boss store where he bought a black, lamb's wool jumper and a German-style, waterproof jacket.

Twenty minutes in a taxi took him to the four star, Coniston Castle Hotel, a rambling red sandstone monument to Victorian wealth, sitting on the edge of a middle class estate of carefully tended bungalows. The hotel had been recently transformed for the twenty-first century with lots of glass panels and subdued lighting, making it one of the most popular wedding venues in the city. There won't be many people looking for a jihadist here, thought Yousef.

In a quiet side street, just off Temple Bar, in the centre of Dublin is a narrow, four-story, plain looking, grey-coloured, concrete building. The brass plaque outside reads 'B.P. transport and Infrastructure Ltd.' On one side of the plaque is shown the familiar, modern, green, B.P. logo and on the other side another, less familiar, logo contained the letters B.P. and T.I.

In Dublin it was an open secret that this was the headquarters of British Intelligence in the Irish Republic. In fact this address was so well known that the joke in the office was, if you got into a taxi anywhere in Ireland and ask to be taken to M.I.6, you would be dropped off at the front door.

The fortunes and purpose of this organisation had changed a lot over the years. At one time it had been home to an extensive network of spies and informants watching the I.R.A. and any sympathisers and fundraisers in the Republic. Later, it became the centre for co-operation between the two governments and as a link to the G.C.H.Q. information centre in Cheltenham, England. Recently almost all the activity has centred on watching the disproportionate number of Irish people travelling to Syria, with a secondary mission to observe and report back on the Irish government's secret links to Russia's President Putin and their tacit support for his interests and activities in the Ukraine.

As Yousef was getting comfortable in the Coniston Castle hotel, a dark blue, Dublin registered, Ford Mondeo dropped off two casually dressed B.P.T.I. personnel at the Dublin Airport Security centre on the eastern edge of the airport campus. Their purpose was to recover and copy the tapes from the security cameras located at the customs entry points together with those from the public areas, filmed during the last four hours. As B.P.T.I. had limited resources, the nine C.D.s that the two security operatives had copied were put into a padlocked, sailcloth, diplomatic bag and spirited across the runway in a small airport van, to be hand delivered to the captain of an Aer Lingus regional jet whose passengers were anxious to get on their way to Birmingham International airport. Yousef's email had been sent to a well-known and considered senior, Jihad financier and had triggered an immediate response from the operations rooms of both the U.K. and U.S. security teams.

***

In Molinos Ridge, Achmed wanted to check out his new rifle. They had not been able to test it on the way up and he wanted to do a test firing and make sure that any adjustments required were already made before Yousef arrived and the gun might need to be used. Not knowing the area, Achmed went to the hotel reception for advice, first making sure it was staffed by someone other than the inquisitive man who had previously checked him in.

"Well if you drive about twelve miles east, going out of town on this road," the receptionist said pointing at a map on the wall, "You will come to a big red and white sign for the Double Horseshoe legalised brothel. Keep on going past that sign until you see another small hanging sign pointing you up a left fork to Wilders farm. The farm is owned by my cousins and I'll phone right now to say that you're coming out and they'll let you use the family's shooting range. Just give him my thanks and twenty dollars and you can shoot there all day. It's real quiet so no-one will disturb you."

"Would it be O.K. if my sister came with and did a bit of shooting too?" enquired Achmed.

"Sure she can. We positively encourage women to be able to shoot well around here. Why, more than half the members of the N.R.A. in this County are women, these days. Would you want us to make you up a box lunch; a bit of ham and cheese perhaps and a couple of beers?"

Achmed politely declined the offer of a lunch box and headed back upstairs to get Noor, some fresh humus, a thermos flask of sweet tea and the car keys for the Chevy.

Rose Culzean returned to the Sheriff's office after comforting Mrs. Bernstein at the Union Hotel, just in time to answer the phone ringing in Carlton's office.

"No, he's gone out but you can get him on his cell phone. That's quick for a ballistic report. Yeah, I'm just writing it down now and I'll tell him just as soon as I see him. That is an unusual weapon. I guess none of us saw that coming. Yes, very funny, the victim sure did see it coming on account of it blowing off half the back of his head. Yes, thanks again for a quick result."

Rose looked down at her note that she had just written. A .44-40 Winchester or else a replica Henry 1860. Now who did she know who had a working version of a gun like that? Rose decided to go over to the doctor's surgery to see if the Doc had enough time for something to eat, a conversation about antique guns and, if they were both in the mood, a bit of 'comfort' on the treatment couch in his surgery, with the front door locked and all the blinds drawn.

CHAPTER 20

In her office in Elisabeth, all the talk was of an important prestige listing. An old three story mill building which had been converted into ten, luxury, five bedroom apartments with European fittings and interior designs by Jean-Claude Breton, who had flown in from Paris to take personal charge of the finished product, was about to be marketed across the whole east coast. Jools had negotiated her way to becoming the sole agent and had press, radio and T.V. advertising to organise, along with a celebrity champagne launch party, in less than two weeks' time. Despite the pressures on her and her staff, all she could think of was how, when and where she was going to tell Alistair about Belfast and what his reaction was going to be when he heard. She decided that to delay any longer would be wrong. What if the English press looking for his crazy brother found out and confronted him? That would be a disaster. She summoned her small staff into her glass-fronted private office and, as they all enjoyed a cup of good strong Rombouts coffee and a few chocolate chip cookies, she spoke to them.

"Some of you have, in the past, told me that I am far too hands on and I should be more trusting and make better use of your individual skills. Well, you are all about to get your chance. I'm going to be away for a couple of days, from tomorrow and I am leaving this office and the new Royale Court development project entirely in your capable hands. You can get me on my smart phone at all times and by Skype on my I pad in the evenings. Each of you knows your own tasks and this is your opportunity to show me what you can do. Help each other and call me only if you get stuck. I am going home to pack a case and arrange for my boys to be looked after. I'll be on the cell phone in my car for another hour. Good luck everyone," and with that said she gathered her things, jumped into her Porsche and sped off.

"Bernice, I'm thinking of joining Alistair for a surprise short visit. Where is he just now and could you email me his schedule?"

"He's in Carson City at the moment and will be south of L.A. for a couple more days. Carson City is a really nice place for a short holiday at this time of year, but he'll be flying out in just a few hours." Bernice sent Jools Alistair's travel agenda to her smartphone as Jools roared home pushing the Porsche along the turnpike road with a determined look in her bright eyes. While doing so, she gave her wrists and the back of her head the occasional nervous squirt of Chanel No.5 perfume, as she drove.

***

"I'm calling this the silver dollar special," announced Big Jim as the wraps came off the new coupe. It was bright silver in colour, had chrome alloy wheels and a two-tone, dark grey and white leather interior. After a short round of applause, Alistair mingled with the crowd and took part in the mock casino games. Armed with the obviously fake money that he'd brought with him from the New York office, he, along with the local customers, stood playing at the genuine, 'Reno style', roulette wheels that had been specially set up in the showroom. He put back into the game the many prizes he was winning, much to his own embarrassment.

"I guess I've always been lucky," announced a slightly red-faced Alistair.

"Nothing wrong with that," bellowed Big Jim from across the roof of the Coupe. Alistair decided to give his good luck a rest and neatly folded ten thousand toy dollars in high bills into his back pocket and stood outside in front of the showroom for some air.

"Ready for the meal of your life?" asked Big Jim, with an even bigger than usual grin on his face.

"You lead, I'll follow," replied Alistair as he slumped back into the soft front seat of Jim's white Lincoln and instinctively opened his window an inch to mix the cigar smoke filled interior with some fresh mountain air.

Even though the Little Amsterdam Restaurant was on a main street in town it resembled a ranch building. Constructed entirely out of wood, the triangular shaped roof hung low on either side of the structure. The inside was just as quirky. The ceiling was made up entirely of branches of various types of fir tree giving the place a lovely natural pine smell. Hanging from the branches was a variety of small lights and glass ornaments.

"What do you think?" asked Big Jim.

"Lovely. A bit like living inside a giant Christmas tree," commented Alistair.

"I knew you would like it. Your P.A. in New York told me that you're a family man, like me. I once had a representative visit me and you'll never guess what he asked me for?"

"What did he ask?"

"He asked me if I could recommend one of the twenty-eight legalised brothels we have here in Nevada!"

"What did you do?" asked Alistair.

"I threw him off my premises then phoned his boss and told him never to send that man to my place ever again, and then I told him why!"

"That must have gone down well," replied Alistair.

"Well to be honest, I couldn't care either way. But when your P.A. Bernice told me about you, your lady wife and your two boys, and you being a Christian, I knew I would enjoy bringing you here for the best meal in the State of Nevada."

***

At Carson City airport, a big, brown UPS van pulled up alongside Jed's small aircraft. The driver was accompanied by the branch manager, who had joined the delivery to meet up with his old friend.

"So what have you got for me this time, you old rascal?" asked Jed.

"Just a few bottles of Nitro Glycerine. Mind you, don't shake them up any, or Kaboom!" joked the manager.

"O.K., less of the fun, what have you really got for me?"

"Fifteen small wooden cases containing spare parts for the big telescope up at the Millers Mountain observatory."

Jed carefully checked out the labels on the little boxes, working out the total weight and where on the aircraft he would place them. Some he put into a thick, builder's sack and strapped them into one of the four seats with the seatbelt provided. The rest were spread carefully on the floor at the rear of the aircraft, then held safely in place, under a piece of thick corrugated cardboard tied down with a couple of colourful, stretchy, hook ended, ties.

***

Alistair tried to contact Jools, using his cell phone, before his special meal with Big Jim got underway. Getting her answering service, he left a short message. "Hi Darling. I'm sorry I missed you. Big Jim and I are just about to eat. Everything's going well. Big Jim's great company. Just what you'd expect. The kind of guy you want in your corner when the chips are down. Speaking of chips, I'm starving, so I'm going to eat now. Call me later if you can. I'm up at the local airport after this. I love you."

Alistair had taken Jim's advice and eaten very little of the food on offer at the showroom, even though it looked and smelled really delicious. As the two men ordered drinks the waiter casually asked Jim, "Is this the gentleman having the meal of his life?" Big Jim nodded and with that two waiters appeared, one at each of Alistair's shoulders, pushing into place on either side, two separate wheeled tables, set up to cook and present food in the flambé style.

"One each?" questioned Alistair.

"No son. They're both for you. I'm getting served from the normal menu. All of this is just for you."

Next to appear was Alistair's special menu. This consisted of a large, flat board in the shape and style of a traditional five storey, Amsterdam merchant's house. The kind you see in postcard photographs, standing in front of a canal. This very unusual menu was about two and a half feet tall, a foot wide and was around an eighth of an inch thick. The doors and all the windows were a bit like those on an advent calendar in that each little flap, when opened, revealed a new dish which the waiters dutifully prepared in front of Alistair. One cooked as one served keeping the whole process up, all night if need be.

"I told you you'd like it," said big Jim as Alistair started his gastronomic journey up the wooden house starting with the front door. Freshwater prawn and avocado in 'our own' thousand island sauce was behind the little flap that made a door. The first window revealed Aberdeen Angus fillet steak, cooked butterfly style, in a vintage Cognac and fresh truffle sauce. Each window was more delicious than the last. All washed down with lots of Carson City's deceptively strong, finest High Sierra, honey ale.

As Alistair neared the top of the house he became more and more full. As he tried to put a small piece of 'pioneer' apple pie with thick custard, laced with Russian vodka and cinnamon into his mouth, he said, "That's it. I can't eat another bite."

Big Jim said, "You did great, Son. Now the boys are going to take a photo of you having the last bite of the meal of your life." At that moment one of the waiters produced a silver Nikon compact camera from his pocket and, saying the words 'face book', snapped Alistair putting his spoon near, but not in his, by now well-stuffed, mouth.

***

As the lights were dimmed in the conference room at B.P.T.I. in central Dublin the six permanent staff and the director took their seats in front of the big screen.

"Would anyone like to tell me who this is?" asked the director, a photo showing the front of the Dublin Airport E.U. customs booth with Yousef appeared on the screen, standing side by side with Sheila and her kids.

"Jihadi Mick?"

"Yes, well done, I am glad to see at least one of you watches the news now and again."

"Who's that with him?" asked one of the staff.

"We think she's just a patsy he picked up along the way, but just in case, the local Garda in Oldcastle, are on their way to arrest her and tear her house apart. A night or two in a cell, away from her children, should teach her not to talk to strangers in future."

"What about our Micky boy, where is he now?"

"That's what you are going to find out, and quickly. We don't want you to approach him or take him into our custody. The press think he's dead and we want him to remain dead. We just want you to find him. I have other plans for removing him from circulation, once I know his whereabouts. What I have planned for him next is on a strictly need to know basis and right now you don't need to know. Here are six files containing the six assignments. Each file has one of your names on it. Usual rules apply. Take your file, get moving and good hunting!"

***

"You're cutting it a bit close," said Jed, looking at his black, Casio pilot's watch. Alistair waved goodbye to Big Jim and turned to hand his suitcase and briefcase to Jed to load into the small plane.

"Yes, I'm sorry. Just a bit too much western hospitality, it was hard to get away.

"My host was cheering me up, telling tales of crashes and disappearances in the Nevada triangle. I'm glad I'm with such an experienced pilot in a new plane," said Alistair, trying to get Jed back on his side for the journey.

"Well, that's kind of you to say, but he was right. This area can kick back any time it likes. The weather for our route tonight looks fine but I've seen it change in an instant. That's why it's important to leave on time."

Alistair helped Jed wedge his favourite, and

expensive, Mont Blanc, leather briefcase in behind his seat. It containing his wallet, I.D, mobile and laptop. Then he strapped himself in tightly ready for take-off.

As they headed off to join the main runway, as if to emphasise Jed's point, some light drizzle began to fall on the plane through the sunshine, causing a rainbow to form.

CHAPTER 21

Rose paid an official visit to Molinos Ridge Hardware, which doubled up as the local gun store, to follow up the lead from ballistics. Almost everyone in the surrounding farms and businesses in the area had at least one gun although most of them remained unfired from one year to the next. From the hardware store owner's carefully hand written records, Rose found three customers who had bought ammunition for antique Winchester type rifles in the last six months. One of the old guys named had since died and that posed the question, where was his gun now? The other two were also pensioners. One owner had been brought to their attention, just a few months before, when he got angry at all the noise the geologists were making, and her brother had to step in before he caused any real trouble. The last name on the list was already a recent entry in her notebook, Mrs Napier.

Rose slowly read aloud her address, "Silver Stream Farm, Molinos Ridge." This was the woman who spoke up at the town meeting when the oilman didn't turn; the one whom Rose had talked to on the phone at the hotel, soon after they found Mr Bernstein lying dead in his car close to the entrance to Mrs Napier's driveway. Rose recognised there were three good possibilities to follow up, but Mrs Napier went straight to the top of the class as she now had three connections with the deceased, and all of Rose's training pointed to her being a person of primary interest in the case. Rose marked everything up on the big blackboard in the Sheriff's office before trying to raise Carlton on his cell phone to give him the news of what she had uncovered.

***

Yousef normally slept well but this time his sleep was disturbed by a constantly running nose and occasional giant sneezes which threw his head forward. He dressed and went down to reception to see if they had anything for a cold.

The receptionist looked genuinely sorry when she told him, "We don't even keep a first aid kit anymore. Funnily enough, it's all to do with health and safety. If I was to give you any medicine and it didn't agree with you, then you might sue the hotel. At least that's the theory anyway. The good news is that there is a really good chemist open nearby and they'll have everything you might want."

Yousef wrapped up warm in his smart new black jumper and waterproof jacket. He marched in misery down the street to the nearby branch of Hickeys Pharmacy, using the directions he had been given. While he was away at the chemist shop buying Lem-sip and throat lozenges, two men, one an inspector from the Garda and one from the Irish security service, sat in the hotel lounge watching the front door. The first had his hand on a mobile phone ready to start a call as an alarm. While a third, a young Englishman from BPIT, quietly entered Yousef's room and searched his belongings before dropping a small device the size of a garden pea through a zip and into the space between the lining and the outside of his suitcase.

Yousef didn't notice the three well-dressed men leaving the hotel as he arrived back. He was on a mission that involved boiling a kettle and using more of the open box of Kleenex in his room. After interviewing the chemist and examining the money that Yousef had handed over, the three men split up, with the Englishman returning to his Temple Bar office to report his findings and activate the device.

The BPTI Director was jubilant as he spoke on the phone. "Yes it is confirmed, we're 110% sure. I know your boss has been looking for him for a long, long time. No we don't want any of the reward. A nice bottle of Malt, next time I'm in Cookstown will do fine. All we ask is that he is never seen or heard of again. According to our files he's already dead and that's how we want you to keep it. Yes, nice and tidy. We now have an electronic tail on him, but we don't expect him to be going anywhere soon."

"It seems the poor lamb caught a cold coming back from Cyprus on a holiday flight. No, only one person and we've just put the fear of God into her. She won't talk about him ever again. Yeah, I've emailed the address and directions, so as soon as you guys arrive we'll give you all the space you need. The Irish Garda is happy to stay out of your way all the way back to the border and we'll keep you safe and undisturbed from there on. About three to four hours? That will be great, thanks."

***

As the small plane soared over the flat calm lake below, Alistair yawned. "Sorry, too much good food and drink and not enough sleep."

Jed Replied, "I'm a bit envious. All I've eaten today is a little bit of breakfast and an apple. I've had plenty to drink though. Only water you'll be glad to hear."

Alistair had full confidence in his pilot and the new plane so he decided to use the time to catch up on some much needed sleep. He thought he might have the start of a cold coming on. Or was it just the tasty, but quite strong local beer his host had been pouring for him all through his meal. Alistair didn't know how long he was out for, but he awoke with a jolt.

The plane was in a steep dive and Jed was slumped unconscious over the controls. It seemed like it had taken only a micro-second for Alistair to come to and take the controls, but the aircraft had already lost most of its altitude and was tumbling towards a dried river bed, strewn with heavy boulders and rocks. Grabbing the controls caused the plane to lean sharply to starboard before starting to straighten up. Alistair managed to regain some measure of control before the tip of the wing made contact with the top of a tree and the whole aircraft flipped over, slid, and eventually ground to a crushing halt. Alistair remained conscious until the last seconds before the impact. He just had enough time to decide, that's the last time I go flying with a diabetic who hasn't eaten, when all the lights in his head went out. When he regained consciousness the whole world was upside down, or at least that's how it seemed. He was still in his seat and hanging by his seatbelt in the badly damaged cabin. He felt sick and could feel blood running along the side of his face from a cut on his head. More worrying was that Jed wasn't breathing and the whole plane reeked of the sweet pungent smell of aviation fuel. Alistair had no time to think and, bracing himself for a fall, opened his seatbelt, and 'fell' upwards banging his already injured head on the twisted roof of the cabin. Somehow, he managed to right himself by standing on the headlining then crawled over Jed. He needed to use all of his strength to open the pilot's door and then deliberately fall out onto the rocky ground.

Fearing an explosion from the fuel-soaked plane, he half walked, half ran along the edge of the dried up river, initially just wanting to escape, but later he began looking out for other dangers and also for signs of civilisation.

He had no idea where he was. Jed could have been unconscious for ages before the plane started to dive, and having a two hundred miles per hour top speed, he could be anywhere in a three to four hundred mile circle thought Alistair. It was starting to get late and going back to the plane, even if he could find it, didn't seem like a good option. After another hour of walking Alistair came across a two lane tarmac country road. If I had a coin I would flip it, but I left everything back at the wreck, he thought as he tried to decide which direction to walk in. He thought he could just about make out the white glow of some lights off in the distance near the horizon, so he turned left and began to walk towards them.

After what seemed like a lifetime Alistair found himself standing in front of a large, yellow, red and white road sign. Madam Butterfly licensed Brothel. Open 24 Hours. Next to the sign was a big red arrow pointing down a long narrow lane. There he was, with a bashed head, no money, covered in blood and stinking of fuel and probably still with a whiff of beer on his breath.

There was no sign of lights down the lane and. even if there was, Alistair wasn't sure what sort of welcome he would get in his present state, so he decided to keep on walking and hopefully he would find a town with a doctor or at the very least a phone. His head hurt and occasionally he found himself drifting in and out of consciousness, as his legs carried him relentlessly forward.

***

Yousef's cold wasn't getting any better. The Lem-sip had momentarily taken the edge off it, but the walk to the pharmacy only seemed to have made it worse in his eyes. Either way, he was feeling miserable and decided he was too unwell to face going down to eat so he had a look at the room service menu instead. Within half an hour there was a knock on his door.

"Room Service!" A tall thin man carried a wide metal tray into the middle of the room. As Yousef turned to follow him in, two other men barged in and pushed him to the ground. The two men held him down while the 'waiter' took a syringe from under a dishcloth covering the tray and injected him with its contents. The last thing Yousef remembered were the three men passing round a plate and helping themselves to his sandwiches as he passed out.

Yousef awoke on the hard plywood floor of a white Ford transit van, travelling at speed and bouncing its way through narrow country roads. He had a bit of duct tape over his mouth and his hands and feet were tightly tied.

"Not so tough now, Mr Jihadi," said one of the three men in the front seats, who had noticed his eyes were open.

"I guess you'll be wondering who's got you and where you're going. Well you'll have guessed from the accent that we are not the Americans, nor are we that old oxymoron, Irish Intelligence, but we will give you a clue. This van is taking you to Cookstown. Cast your mind back to the last time you were in our town."

Yousef remembered that the only time he had been in Cookstown was many years ago. He was the driver on a raid on a Sub Post office, but what could that possibly have to do with his abduction from the Republic? Was this the Police service of Northern Ireland out on a flyer? He wondered, as the van continued its progress at a slightly reduced pace.

"Take his gag off. I want to hear what he has to say," said the van driver, who was a thick-set man with a strong Belfast accent and even stronger body odour.

"So who are you then and what's this all about?" asked Yousef genuinely confused, still full of the cold and a bit groggy from his drug fuelled slumber.

"You might describe us as private contractors," replied the third man, who up until then had not spoken.

"Do you remember when you left the post office in the stolen Jag?" Yousef nodded. "You hit a woman pushing a pram on the crossing outside the library?" he nodded again, even though it had meant nothing to him at the time.

"Well the lady ended up in a wheelchair and the baby died. Her husband, a very prominent man in loyalist circles, put up a £30,000 reward to bring you back here. You see he would like to talk to you. That's where you're going, once we have arranged for him to give us the money in cash."

The van pulled up in front of a traditional one and a half storey, white, smallholding house beside an old, 'Atcost' barn with a corrugated tin roof and with a wall of hay neatly stacked inside. Yousef was led into the barn and chained to a thick metal post. The driver then punched him hard in the face. "That's for being a Catholic," and then kicked him even harder between the legs. "And that's for being a Moslem. We don't get many like you who are both, but that just makes you two different types of vermin in my book."

Yousef knew that he wasn't going to get any sympathy or even reasonably civilised treatment from the men or from their business associate.

Still it could be worse, he thought. If the roles were reversed he would have done a lot more to them by now just for the sheer pleasure it would give him.

CHAPTER 22

Jools was always in a hurry at an airport although she always left more than enough time to go through the many stages modern travel demands. But, it was her competitive nature that came out. She had to be first in any queue, first on the plane, first off the plane, first at the luggage belt.

Her exit from L.A.X was no different. She only stopped momentarily, to restart her cell phone as she fought her way at full speed towards the car hire desk to pick up her pre-booked compact model.

Fourteen emails and one SMS text message.

The text was from Bernice, Alistair's P.A. and it read:

URGENT, Hi Jools, please call me immediately you get this message. It's important. Bernice.

Jools had never had a message like it from a normally deferential and quite 'wordy' Bernice, so she stopped what she was doing and stood in the middle of the connecting tunnel with all the other passengers overtaking her, to call Bernice and find out, 'where's the fire?'

Bernice had been crying for over an hour, but held it together just long enough to talk to Jools in as calm a voice as she could muster. "It's about Alistair's plane," she said. "The light plane taking him from Carson City. It didn't return to the airfield when it was meant to and it's now several hours late. All the authorities know about it, in fact they called me. They've probably put down safely on another airstrip or a golf course or something, but I thought you should know right away."

"I want you to give the authorities my cell phone number and then get me the address and phone number for the man Alistair calls Big Jim. The last place we know for sure he was is Carson City and I'm on my way there now. Call me if you hear anything else."

At first, Jools was too shocked and too surprised to really take in what was happening. Here she was halfway across the country on her way to meet a husband who might already be dead. No, she mustn't think like that. God couldn't possibly be so cruel as to make her a widow twice in her short life.

Not her God.

She tried Alistair's mobile phone. Three rings. "Thank you for calling Alistair McKenzie of Ford Motor Company. I'm unable to..."

Jools stopped the message. Perhaps Bernice might be right. Maybe they had safely brought the little plane down on a golf course and he was, at this very moment, propping up the bar on the nineteenth hole with a gin and tonic in his hand, before booking a taxi., Meanwhile half the world, including Jools, was worried sick about him.

One thing was certain. She wasn't going to find

him by hanging around the arrivals lounge at the airport.

"Julia McKenzie, pull yourself together," she said to herself.

She took her large bottle of Chanel No.5, eau de parfum, from the outside pocket of her suitcase, put a couple of squirts on her wrists and the back of her neck, straightened up and took on the air of authority and strength that her husband so admired. The one that her children and her staff at work had come to learn they could always rely on.

Jools strode to the hire car desk, walking even quicker than usual with her strong heart running true and fast. "I have a reservation for an economy car, but I want you to amend it. What have you got that's fast?"

After a quick run through of her special edition, 'ultimate' AMEX card, she was shown out to the hire car lot, where a very low mileage, metallic blue, Dodge Challenger was waiting. After taking a few moments to link her smartphone to the car's Bluetooth system and putting the co-ordinates of the Ford dealership in Carson City into the on-board satellite navigation system, Jools pressed down on the gas and the powerful car bounded out of the parking lot and on towards the interstate.

***

Alistair walked and walked for what felt like a lifetime. Eventually he found himself leaning on a grey metal post which was holding up a sign, next to the road.

Welcome to
Molinos Ridge.
Elevation 3464

Alistair had never heard of the place, but right now it could have been called 'salvation' as that's what it felt like to him.

Using up his last bit of energy, his tired feet carried him into town. As he stood in the middle of the road the deputy sheriff's car pulled up beside him and Rose stepped out.

"Put your hands on the car and assume the position," said Rose with polished authority, assuming he was one of the bums from the makeshift trailer camp two miles out of town. The Sheriff's department had warned them, on more than one occasion, to stay out of town or get arrested. Then she noticed the expensive black leather shoes and his gold Rolex watch."

"What in hells name happened to you?" asked Rose.

"I was in some kind of an accident," replied Alistair.

"You sure look it, what's your name Mister?"

Alistair stopped and thought. Then he thought a bit harder. It was a simple enough question and there was no reason why he couldn't answer. It was only that the filling cabinet in his head where he kept that information was locked and no matter how he tried to open it, the lock just would not budge. While Alistair stood looking into space Rose realised he might need medical attention. The Doc was out of town for the rest of the day so it became her responsibility, as she saw it, to look after him.

"Get in the vehicle. I'm taking you to my office to clean you up. You can have a sleep in an open cell until the doc gets back. I'll buy you some food and coffee right now which you can have when you're ready."

Rose stopped at the Deli on the way to pick up some coffee, bagels and some cheese.

She leaned through the open window of her car and asked, "Is this all right for you or would you like something else?"

Alistair replied, "Thanks but I'm not very hungry right now." Rose drove the short distance to her office and putting her arm under Alistair's shoulder helped him up the ramp to the office.

"This is very good of you," said Alistair, squinting at her kind face and seeing her dyed-blonde hair shimmering in the sunlight.

"All part of the service, Mister," replied Rose, helping him as he stumbled the last few steps into the building.

***

Jools phoned ahead and told Big Jim what had happened. After the initial shock, he said, "I'd like you to come here first and we can both look for him together. I'll make a start on the phone and begin to gather some gear we might need."

Jools replied, "Alistair said you were a great guy to have around in a crisis. I guess he was right."

"Your husband told me a lot of good things about you too. Now don't you worry little lady, we'll find your husband all right or my names not Big Jim. Just you get here safe and it will all be okay."

***

Noor hurried back to the Hotel from her food shopping trip to the Molinos Ridge Deli.

"Achmed, he's here! That boy in the Deli, the one who likes me, said the deputy sheriff woman had him in her car and forced him into the Sheriff's office holding a gun in his back. He said he thinks he got arrested for killing the big Jewish oilman."

"Well that certainly sounds like our man. Are you sure it is him?" questioned Achmed.

"Very sure. His description is an exact match, right down to the Northern Ireland accent and the flashy watch."

Achmed thought long and hard then said, "Let's get our guns. We need to bust him out of there before the FBI turn up and make it impossible. We'll not get very far, walking in, all guns blazing. What I'll do is become a sniper. I'll hide across the street with the rifle and you hide round the side of the office and we can pick them off. If we succeed it will then become easy for us to go in and rescue Yousef."

When Sheriff Culzean returned to his office, Rose was on the phone to the Doc.

"Yeah, he's taken a pretty hard crack on the head and he has a nasty cut above his right eye. I cleaned him up and put a plaster over the cut. He smelled strongly of something like paraffin, but not paraffin. Perhaps it was lubricating oil of some kind. Also, I could tell he'd been drinking. I could smell it on his breath. No, he's still not able to tell me much. He touched my hair and remembered a name, Felice, maybe that's his wife or daughter's name. He's wearing a valuable wedding ring along with the gold Rolex I told you about, so he is married.

"Yeah, as soon as possible. We'll bring him across."

***

Yousef started to feel better. The sun had begun to come out and his cold was no longer troubling him as much. He didn't know how long he'd been in the barn as the driver had taken Schneider's watch along with his other possessions from the hotel room before calmly paying the bill with some of Yousef's cash and checking out. Yousef decided that this was a good time to pray. He started by giving thanks for the two most recent times he'd been spared before going through a more formal ritual, kneeling on the ground at the end of a chain, like an animal, he thought.

For many months he'd prepared himself for martyrdom. It seemed ironic that after giving so much for his cause he would eventually die for something he considered to be of no importance and which had happened long before he became a Muslim. Perhaps, if he had discovered his true faith earlier, he would not have found himself in this position.

Just as he thought about his fate, an old woman came out of the farmhouse carrying a mug of tea and a side plate with some Tunnock's Caramel Wafer's. She entered the barn and saying nothing to Yousef placed the mug and the plate on the ground beside him before returning in silence to the house. The hot strong tea and biscuits were very welcome and he quickly attributed this simple act of kindness to the prayers he had just completed. He thought about the old woman and his captors and what a strange place Northern Ireland really was. So much anger and religious bigotry wrapped up in the other side of religion, namely kindness and forgiveness. It sure was an odd place to grow up in especially in the middle of 'the troubles', as he had.

***

Jools finished her long and illegally fast journey and pulled into the garage. She could see a great big man standing in the middle of the showroom waving his arms as several other people were running about. It looked to her as though they were being chased by a lion.

"Hurry up, she could be here at any moment and we need to be ready to rock and roll right away," shouted Big Jim at his small group of now exhausted workers as they loaded up a big yellow and black 4x4, which was pointing out through the open showroom's full-height window in anticipation of a quick getaway.

"Are you Jools?"

She nodded, then quite suddenly and unexpectedly Big Jim locked her in a huge bear hug that almost caused her to stop breathing.

"I'm glad you're here safe; you don't need to worry any. I've thought of everything and, if you're up to it, we're ready to go right now and find that nice husband of yours."

Big Jim walked her over to the 4X4.

"This is a special edition Ford F150 Raptor, with the biggest, most powerful engine in the range. In the tail is a luxury two-bedroom tent, a full medical kit, a stretcher, climbing rope and enough food and supplies to last a week. Inside there's a whole lot of the latest communication equipment including a loudspeaker for calling out his name. In the cabin is a gun rack with two big calibre pump action shotguns, in case of trouble. You can use a gun, can't you?" asked Big Jim.

"My folks brought me up to be able to look after myself. My daddy was the NRA state shooting champion for 1978 and 81. And I've won the shield, as ladies champion, for the last two years in a row."

"Damn, that husband of yours sure picked a good one. Any more like you at home?"

"Only my three big brothers and they're all spoken for. Where do you think we should start the search?"

"They could be almost anywhere, but I have a hunch that if we start our search here at a place called Molinos Ridge," he said pointing on the map, "It will place us pretty close to the centre of the search area and the shortest distance to travel if we get a call."

"Molinos Ridge it is then, and don't spare the horses."

"Yes Ma'am," said Big Jim as he took to the controls of the full size 4x4 and waved to his staff with his big, beige coloured cowboy hat through the open car window, in true wild west style, as he drove off.

CHAPTER 23

Yousef watched as the white transit van that had brought him from Dublin parked at the farm house. There seemed to be a meeting going on. A bit of shouting resulted in one man walking away down the path looking very angry and the two other men coming forward to talk to him.

"You're a lucky bastard," said the man who had punched and kicked him earlier. "Turns out the price on your head has been withdrawn. It seems you're not the only one round here that's gone and got religion.

"They say it's good to forgive, but not when there's thirty grand at stake," said the other man.

"What's going to happen to me now?" asked Yousef.

"You're going to join a very special organisation. The double dead club."

You see the Americans think they've killed you and now the English think we've killed you. If I were you, I would stay dead for a long, long time. In fact, stay double dead if you can. We've got your 17,000 euros, all that Turkish dosh, your flash watch, your smart jacket and your laptop and phone. We're also keeping your dirty photos and your cash and stuff will pay for our inconvenience and your catering bill. We'll drop you in town and, just to show that we're not ungrateful, we'll give you twenty quid and an old coat to help you get out of here.

"Now remember what we said. Don't hang about Cookstown and make sure you stay dead, or else everyone on the planet will be after you, including us."

***

Carlton and Rose helped Alastair up on to his feet. He was still a bit shaky but could now walk if a bit unsteadily. He'd managed to eat a little and the hot coffee they'd given him was really welcome.

"We're going to walk you over to the hotel. The doctor's agreed to meet us there and he can have a look at you. The hotel will advance you a room for the night using your watch as security and by then we hope to know who you are and find your friends and family to take you home. Is that all right?"

Alistair thanked them for their help and consideration. As Carlton walked out the front door and down the disabled ramp ahead of Alistair and Rose, he caught sight of what he thought was the glint of a reflection coming from beside the trash cans across the street. His right hand was in his pocket trying to separate a chiclet of cinnamon chewing gum from its packet. He immediately dropped the chewing gum down into the pocket and instinctively reached up for his pistol. Before his hand could reach the mother of pearl handle a rifle bullet passed half an inch under his left eye and exploded in his head. He was dead before he reached the ground.

Rose followed her training and her first thought was for Alistair and, as she threw him to the ground, Noor stepped out from behind her and shot her once in her left leg and shot her again this time grazing her in the head with sufficient force to temporarily knock her out.

Then Noor grabbed Alistair and ran him down the ramp to the waiting car were Achmed had now jumped into the driving seat and was revving the engine. Defying excruciating pain, Rose momentarily regained consciousness just long enough to fire a single shot, putting a slow puncture into the back tire of the white Chevy before her head injury returned her to darkness. She came too with the doc cradling her in his arms.

"Thank God, for a moment I thought I'd lost you," said the doc.

"Carlton, is he?"

"I'm sorry, Darling, he's gone."

Rose gripped the doc's hand tight as she tried to take in what she had just heard. For the first time since being shot she was not aware of being in pain, well not physical pain at least. She felt so very alone. Carlton had always been there for her, even when she worked in L.A. he always told her, "if things get too rough, you can always come home," and home to Rose meant family as much as her little town in Nevada.

For a moment, as the doc comforted her by brushing her blonde hair back and running his warn hand gently across her brow, Rose thought about a trip she and Carlton had made as children. They'd travelled to a rented beachside holiday house in Santa Monica, with the two of them in the back seat of her dad's big old Buick. That was the most comfortable car in the world and the best summer of their lives. As a single, heavy tear left her eye and ran down her face and under her chin Rose symbolically cupped her right hand on her Deputy Sheriff's badge, then transferred her hand to the grip on the handle of her pistol.

As the colour returned to her face, anger bordering on hatred, gradually followed by a strong sense of guilt, began to enter her head. Why had she dismissed so readily the conversation in the Deli about the strangers in town? Had she become too comfortable, too relaxed living in a small town? She wouldn't have ignored a lead like that back in L.A.

Her beloved brother, Carlton was dead and it was all her fault.

She could have picked up the two strangers staying at the Union Hotel at any time and none of this would have happened. Making jokes about foreign food with a couple of cold blooded assassins in town. How could she have been so stupid? Those bastards are going to pay for this, if it's the last thing I do, thought Rose, as anger and adrenaline flooded her injured body with, what felt to her like, the strength of ten men.

The doc had tended to her wounds and stopped any flow of blood.

"Help me get up and fetch me my daddy's gun from Carlton's body."

"Rose, I would not advise that."

"Do as I ask! I'm the sheriff now, not you. The safety of the people of this town is <u>my</u> responsibility. Besides it's what Carlton would want me to do."

***

Yousef was placed, bound with a plastic cable tie, once again in the back of the Ford transit and driven to the edge of the town centre. Then his hands were untied and he was literally kicked out of the van's back door and he landed hard on the wet road. The jacket he was wearing smelled like the unwashed van driver and was at least two sizes too big for him. It didn't take him long to decide his next move. He walked into the reception of the nearest hotel and asked if they had a public phone. He did what he had been taught to do in case of an emergency since having it drummed into him as a small boy. He dialled 100 and asked to make a reverse charge call to a number he knew off by heart.

"Hello, Mammy, it's your son Daniel. No, I'm in Cookstown, Northern Ireland. Could somebody come and get me, I could do with a bath and a meal."

***

Jools and Big Jim missed Alistair and the shooting by only a few minutes, but did arrive in time to talk to Rose as she once again regained consciousness under the care of the doc.

"Is your name Felice?" asked Rose. "No, oh well I must have got that wrong. I got shot in the head and I'm a bit out of it at the moment. Yes, it will be your husband. A light plane crash, which explains the smell. Aviation fuel. Lucky he wasn't blown up."

As the two women spoke, the assistant manager

from the hotel ran up to them, sweat pouring from his brow.

"I saw everything and, as I was returning to work on my Harley, I followed them for a couple of miles to the old disused Shell gas station, just out of town," he said pointing south as he talked. "They had a flat tyre and kept driving. The wheel looks seized onto the car and all three are holed up inside the building."

"We'll go ahead," said Jools, and she pulled Big Jim back to the 4x4 then drove off fast in a cloud of dust before Rose had time to think or try to stop them.

***

"What should we do now, Yousef?" asked Achmed, looking straight into Alistair's eyes.

"I was rather hoping you might know," was his cautious reply. Alistair wasn't sure what had just happened or why. All he knew was that he was in the company of cold blooded killers who thought his name was Yousef. Something he was pretty sure wasn't right.

"I'll bet you I could fix that wheel if only I had the right tools. It just needs a bit of heat applied to it and I could get it to come right off."

"Are you some sort of a mechanic now?" I thought you were a great Jihadist. A leader. Look Noor, it looks like we have risked our lives for a mechanic."

Noor put her arm round her brother, but he brushed her aside.

"Look, all he has in his pockets is $10,000 dollars in toy town money. We've put everything on the line for this." He picked up the bundle of obviously fake, high value, bank notes from the launch party and threw them in the air.

There was a high pitched whine, which was heard all around the building and beyond as Big Jim powered up the broadcast standard P.A. system in the F150 in preparation for Jools beginning to speak.

"This is Mrs. Julia McKenzie. We are heavily armed and have you surrounded. The man you are holding is my husband, Alistair McKenzie. We are not interested in what happened earlier. It has nothing to do with us. Just let Alistair go and we will leave this place and you can go free. We'll even give you our car. Just let Alistair go and it's your ticket out of here and to freedom. The police aren't here yet, so make your mind up quick. Be assured, if you harm Alistair in any way, we will kill you." Jools fired a couple of shots in the air to show she meant business.

"Is your name Alistair McKenzie?"

As Alistair spoke his own name for the first time, in what had seemed like an age to him. It was as though all the closed files in his head suddenly began to spring open. He remembered his home and his beautiful, classic, old, light metallic green Lincoln Continental with its padded vinyl roof and odd shaped opera windows at the rear.

He could once again imagine himself cooking steaks and corn on his traditional, red, Weber barbeque and working on the tiny engine of his model plane in the garden of his New Jersey home, while being watched over with interest and affection by his eldest son Al.

His model plane. Yes a plane. "I was on a plane that crashed!

"I wasn't the pilot. No, I was in the passenger seat up front. It was a four seat single engine job. I got hit from behind by a couple of heavy small wooden boxes and that was really painful. Soon after we hit the ground hard and that's when I must have blacked out."

He started to remember little bits of his experience and his past and then the bits started to join together to make whole memories.

Jed had his eyes open, staring right at me, not moving, he thought. He started to feel concern and sadness for the larger than life, U.S. Air Force hero who had shown kindness and impressed him so much on the outbound journey. At the same time Alistair realised how lucky he had been to survive the crash. All I have to do now is survive this mess, he thought.

"I think Jed is definitely a goner," he heard himself say aloud, much louder than he would have wished.

If the diabetic hypo didn't kill him the crash will have. I don't recall him breathing and we hung upside down together for what must have been quite a while. Still, if I get out of this alive, Jools and I must go and look for him just to make sure, he thought to himself, realising that his deadly companions were not in any way interested in the revelations which were coming increasingly quickly into his recovering mind.

Jools, what's she doing out here, way out west.

And why is she firing her gun? None of this makes sense, thought Alistair.

He knew for certain that he had just witnessed a brutal execution of one law enforcement officer and the serious, perhaps fatal injury of another.

The manner and body language of his two 'liberators' was becoming more and more erratic as the minutes ticked away.

Alistair decided that the best thing to do was to try to stay calm and stay quiet and let Jools take charge. He trusted her judgement completely and while he was trying to get his head straight, he could think of no one else in the world he would rather have on his side, no matter how or why she got there or for that matter, wherever, 'there', might be.

"Okay we are sending him out now. Leave the keys in the car or we will shoot him in the back, got it?"

Alistair did as he was told and very slowly walked away from the gas station and away from Jools, Big Jim and the 4x4.

As he did so, Achmed and Noor ran towards the car. Achmed facing Jools and Noor keeping her gun trained on Alistair. Twenty feet behind Jools and Big Jim, Rose appeared from behind a rock with her own pistol in her left hand and her father's big colt in her right.

She emptied all twelve barrels sharing them equally between Achmed and Noor as they approached, without stopping to draw breath. In an instant it was all over as Jools, followed by Big Jim, ran to help Alistair who had hit the ground, thinking that all the shots were aimed at him.

"That's some girl you've got yourself," said Big Jim, patting Alistair on the shoulder as he got back on to his feet.

"I know," said Alistair. "A real American girl, strong and true, just like I always wanted."

Jools stood behind Alistair and wrapped her arms around him, then showed him her hands and said, "As long as I have these two hands, my love, no one will ever threaten you or anyone in our family, ever again."

***

In Belfast, Brenda was overjoyed to have her son home. "Daniel, I have a lot to tell you. Something that has been hidden from you for your whole life and the time has now come for you to know," she said.

***

As Jools sat in the back of the 4x4 holding hands with Alistair and with Big Jim driving, she said, "Alistair, I have a lot to tell you, it's something that has been hidden from you for your whole life and the time has now come for you to know."

End

Ian Grant

About the author

Ian was trained as an advertising copy writer and worked with the top newspapers and commercial radio stations in his native Scotland. His later career saw him as a key negotiator on multi -million pound engineering contracts in the UK and overseas.

Returning to his first love, writing, Ian has brought his extensive experience of powerful people and stimulating places and combined it with the precision and clarity readily associated with an advertising background to produce a work that is both up to the minute and attention grabbing as well as compelling you to read on.

About Author Way Limited

Author Way provides a broad range of good quality, previously unpublished works and makes them available to the public on multiple formats.

We have a fast growing number of authors who have completed or are in the process of completing their books and preparing them for publication and these will shortly be available.

Please keep checking our website to hear about the latest developments.

Author Way Limited

www.authorway.net